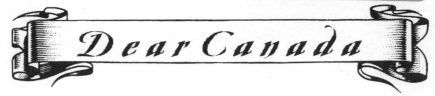

Dear Canada

A Time for Giving

Ten Tales of Christmas

Scholastic Canada Ltd.

Published by Scholastic Canada Ltd.
SCHOLASTIC and DEAR CANADA and logos are trademarks
and/or registered trademarks of Scholastic Inc.

www.scholastic.ca

Library and Archives Canada Cataloguing in Publication

A time for giving : ten tales of Christmas / Jean Little, Sarah Ellis,
Carol Matas, Karleen Bradford, Susan Aihoshi, Barbara Haworth-Attard,
Norah McClintock, Janet McNaughton, Ruby Slipperjack.

(Dear Canada)
Includes nine sequels to previously published Dear Canada titles, and one
prequel to an upcoming title.
Issued in print and electronic formats.
ISBN 978-1-4431-3373-9 (pbk.).—ISBN 978-1-4431-4673-9 (Apple edition).—ISBN
978-1-4431-3374-6 (ebook)

1. Christmas stories, Canadian (English). 2. Children's stories,
Canadian (English). 3. Canada—History—Juvenile fiction. I. Little, Jean,
1932-, author II. Series: Dear Canada

PS8323.C57T56 2015   jC813'.081083271 C2015-901861-7
C2015-901862-5

6 5 4 3 2 1   Printed in Canada 121   15 16 17 18 19

The display type was set in Baskerville.

First printing June 2015

MIX
Paper from
responsible sources
FSC® C004071

Table of Contents

Introduction

Mountains, prairies, seaside . . . Wartime, one hundred and fifty years ago, half a century ago . . . The ten stories in this new Dear Canada Christmas anthology take us all across our land, from remote homesteads to internment camps, from towns destroyed to a city bursting with pride. Set in landscapes of snowflakes and snow angels, wilderness and cozy homes, these stories feature Christmas traditions both familiar and new.

In one of the stories — a departure from exploring our diarists' lives the Christmas *after* — we have the prequel to an upcoming Dear Canada novel: Ojibwe writer Ruby Slipperjack's story of young Violet (Pynut) Pesheens, the Christmas *before* she goes away to Residential School.

I hope you enjoy reconnecting with old friends here, and making some new ones, as you let these young diarists share with you their latest challenges and successes.

Happy Christmas and Happy Reading,
Sandra Bogart Johnston, Editor, Dear Canada Series

Dorothy Wilton

That Fatal Night
The *Titanic* Diary of Dorothy Wilton

Halifax, Nova Scotia
May 1912 – July 1912

BY SARAH ELLIS

It has been over half a year since Dorothy spent time with her grandparents in England, put on plays with Millie and Owen, and had deep discussions with Grandfather — a time that seems far off, given her harrowing voyage aboard the Titanic. *Right now it's nearing Christmas and Dorothy is looking forward to a visit from her big brother Charles and his girlfriend Naomi.*

The Angel of Citadel Hill

December 5, 1912

Today we had a letter from Charles. Mother always saves his letters for me to open when I come home from school so that I can read them first. She knows how much I miss him.

Today's letter had BIG NEWS. Medium-sized surprise: He is coming home for Christmas. This is a surprise because for the past three years he has not had leave from his job over Christmas because he is a junior in the firm and so he hasn't been able to travel from New York all the way to Halifax. (They don't even have Boxing Day as a holiday in the United States, so they only have one day's holiday, which is sad for them.) (Of course, he did come home last spring, to bring me back, but I don't want to write about that.) He couldn't give us much notice because he didn't know about his holidays.

Very large surprise: He is engaged to be married! His fiancée is named Naomi Livingston. (I had to go and ask Mother about the spelling of *fiancée*. It sounds as if it has something to do with finance and it also sounds French, but really it just means a woman who is engaged to be married. He's a fiancé; she's a fiancée.) She is twenty years old. Charles met her at a sailing regatta in the summertime.

Gigantic surprise: Naomi Livingston is coming home with Charles! They will arrive on December 13. Eight days, I can't WAIT.

December 6

By breakfast this morning Mother was already planning for the visit. Father said it was like she was heading a military campaign, and he started to sing a tongue-twister song called "A Modern Major General" until she said, "Father! Settle down," in a very stern tone.

The first thing to be decided was what room Naomi would have. This was a long discussion lasting through porridge as well as toast, but it was mostly Mother discussing with herself. The conclusion was that Naomi would have my room and they would put a cot in the box room for me. I don't mind. I like the box room, which is tiny and cozy and also on the third floor where I think it might be easy to smuggle Borden into the room to sleep with me.

At school I shared the NEWS with Winnifred and Flo. We all agreed that Naomi is the most beautiful name ever. Flo thinks that having a sister-in-law will be just like having a grown-up sister, but much better. Flo has a grown-up sister herself, so she's the expert. I asked why a sister-in-law is better and she said that a grown-up sister remembers having to change your diapers and that makes it impossible for them to ever take you seriously.

This got us all giggling and while we were in the middle of giggling, Winnifred said that Naomi will probably be very sophisticated, being from New York and all, and didn't we all wish we could go to New York sometime. And then Flo said, "Winnifred!" and all the giggling stopped.

I hate this. Winnifred forgot that New York was where I was taken after the *Titanic* disaster. I *like it* that she forgot. I don't want people to always remember and be careful and then go all awkward and apologetic. I don't want to be the one who makes the giggling stop.

December 7

The Major General has become possessed. Since she found out that Naomi is coming, she seems to think that the whole house needs to be taken apart and put back together again. Her favourite word is *shabby*. Last night we were sitting in the parlour just reading when Mother suddenly looked up and said, "Oh, Father, look at the hearth rug. It's so shabby.

What will Naomi think?" Father replied that of course it was shabby because Borden had been sleeping on it. Mother said we had to find a new one right away and Father said wouldn't a good beating do and Mother said certainly not, and Borden, who really should have had the final say, did not contribute to the discussion.

December 9

I am in the box room. Mother calls it sulking. Sulking is a word grown-ups use to keep you from having your say. It is NOT FAIR that when you are a child you are not supposed to talk back *and* you are not supposed to sulk. That's like saying if you're angry you can't keep it in and you can't let it out. What *are* you supposed to do? Sit by and let Mr. Puddlington redecorate your room and cover up your ivy wallpaper?

Back up and report the story properly.

Today, when I got home from school, Mother was in the kitchen with Aunt Hazel and Mr. Puddlington. Father calls Mr. Puddlington the house genius. He sees to the boiler. He knows all about drains and leaky roofs. It turns out that he is also a wallpaper hanger, and he was sitting at the kitchen table with a big book of wallpaper samples. Mother had decided that the wallpaper in my room was "shabby" (of course) and needed to be replaced. She and Aunt Hazel were favouring a pattern called Floral Bouquet.

I said most politely that I was very fond of my ivy wallpaper and that I didn't care to have new. They asked me why I didn't want a "lovely fresh bright new modern pattern." This is when I knew I was doomed. I knew I could not tell them that on my wallpaper all the ivy vines link up. You can lie in bed and travel all around the room and you never take the same route twice. Floral Bouquet is just blobs of flowers. You can't go anywhere on blobs unless you hop like a frog. So I just said that I liked the ivy and wanted to keep it. Then Aunt Hazel said, "Is somebody perhaps just a little jealous of Charles's new sweetheart?" Then I went into a rage so I left the room before I said something bad. That's why I'm in the box room. Sulking.

Later

Father took my side! He came up to see me when he returned from work and he said that it is my room and I am allowed to make decisions about wallpaper. "Your mother is just nervous about meeting Naomi," he said. "Being busy helps her." He then proposed the compromise that we let Mr. Puddlington repaint my woodwork. "Mother thinks a nice cream colour would brighten things up." I like my green wood-work and was getting ready to disagree when Father winked and said, "Concede the battle, Dorothy. You won the war."

December 12

Tomorrow is the big day. I think Mother would like it if we all stopped breathing so as to not dirty up the air.

December 13

Friday the thirteenth is the opposite of unlucky in our house because Naomi is here and she's perfect. She's taller than I expected, nearly as tall as Charles. She has dark brown hair, short and wavy. I love the way she says water — "wohdr" — and coffee — "cahfee." The first thing she said when Mother showed her to my room was, "What a pretty room, I do like the wallpaper," and that made Mother and me both laugh and then Mother told her she would explain later. Even Borden likes her, and he is very particular. She is settling in and soon it will be dinner.

December 14

I think I'm finding out more about what it is like to be in love. Naomi and Charles just exchange these little looks as though there is nothing else in the world, like everything else has disappeared.

For example, this evening Father decided to play some Christmas carols on the mandolin. When he plays "Joy to the World" he makes it sound like a dance number. We all got silly and sang many verses. I noticed that Naomi wasn't singing along. Mother said, "Do you enjoy singing, Naomi?" She gave a big smile and said, "No, I have a complete tin ear. I'm musically hopeless." Then Charles said, "Yes, she couldn't carry a tune in a bucket!" Then he looked at her as though not being able to carry a tune was something so wonderful and special. I always thought that somebody loved somebody else for what they *were* good at. But it also looks like you can love somebody for what they are *not* good at as well. That's a relief.

December 15

Naomi came with presents for everyone. Mine was a polished wooden box with a tortoiseshell tatting shuttle and several colours of tatting cotton. Charles had told her that I know how to crochet, and she said that tatting is even more fun and she's going to teach me to make lace. She was wearing a beautiful lace collar that she made herself.

December 18

I have been too busy to write. In a nutshell, over the past three days we decorated the house and made a wreath. Christmas concert at school. I went shopping with Naomi and I'm trying to finish a tatted doily for Mother's present. Charles brought a newfangled camera with him and he's been taking photographs. His friend Cedric came over and they compared cameras and had long talks about daylight loading and tank development.

We had a Christmas parcel from England with letters. Millie has joined the Girl Guides. My present from Grandmother and Grandfather feels like a book.

December 19

Only one more day of school. Today Winnifred and Flo and Phoebe and I poked along home as slowly as we could. Phoebe says that there is going to be a Girl Guide group starting at the church next spring. We're all going to join. Why should Boy Scouts have all the fun?

When I got home Charles and Naomi had gone out somewhere. Aunt Hazel and Mrs. Hill were over for tea. I passed the tea things and then I settled down under the piano with Borden and my tatting. After they admired my picot stitch they forgot about me. I've noticed that this happens if I sit under the piano. It's a good location for finding out what's going on.

Mother told Auntie and Mrs. Hill all the things she knew about Naomi. Mrs. Hill asked who her people were and Mother said that she is one of the New York Livingstons and that they have an apartment in Manhattan and a summer house on some island or other.

"She rides." Nods from the ladies.

"They sail." More nods.

She reported that Naomi has four brothers and sisters, two older, two younger. "She said she was the ham in the sandwich and then Charles said she was too elegant to be ham and was more like cucumber and cream cheese. Isn't that darling?" The ladies agreed that that was darling.

She forgot to tell them about Naomi's dog. His name is Laird and he loves to swim but now he is quite old and a bit smelly, but nobody in the family minds except her younger sister Priscilla, who can be difficult.

My mind wandered for a minute, but I started to pay attention again when Mother's voice changed. She said that Naomi seemed very close to her family. "I had always assumed that Charles would come back to Halifax some day. Foolish, I know."

Then Aunt Hazel said that when a daughter marries you gain a son, but when a son marries you lose a son. Then everything went very quiet.

Me too. I stopped tatting. I had always figured that even though Charles was in New York learning to be a businessman, his real home was Halifax. I thought that he and Naomi would come and live here. One day. When a brother marries, do you lose a brother?

And what about Grandmother and Grandfather?

When Father married he went to a completely different country, Canada. Maybe that is just what happens.

Sometimes I don't want to grow up.

December 20

I'm in bed and it's late. My light is supposed to be out, but nobody comes and checks on me here in the box room. I can't sleep because I have too much to think about.

This evening Father and Mother went out to the Hills' for dinner, but Charles and Naomi didn't go because Naomi wasn't feeling well. Charles said he would heat up some soup for Naomi and then there was a lot of teasing about whether bachelors could heat up soup without burning it. Naomi said she would so appreciate it if I could stay home as well to keep her company.

As soon as Mother and Father left, however, Naomi made a miracle recovery. We sat in the kitchen to eat and Charles said I was sworn to secrecy, but really it was a white lie and he just couldn't face an evening with the Hills. "Mrs. Hill's all right, but that Rev. Hill! He's just so pompous and boring." I didn't know the word *pompous* before, but he didn't need to explain it. It felt naughty to say something bad about a minister, but also secretly fun.

I told them about the day in confirmation class

when he made Phoebe cry. One of the show-off boys in the class asked Rev. Hill if angels were boys or girls. He said they were neither. Phoebe, who is going to be the angel in the pageant, argued and said if angels weren't girls, why did they have long curly hair and dresses? Then Rev. Hill said that almost everything we thought about angels was just sentimental and that all we knew about them from the Bible was that they are powerful and they come with messages. Then he went on and on about Seraphim and Cherubim and all the different angel kinds in a boring sort of way.

Then Louise, who doesn't usually speak up, said that the other thing we know is that when people die they become angels. And Rev. Hill said that there is no theological reason to believe that. I guess he forgot that Phoebe's nana had just died. Anyway, Phoebe cried and we all started to argue and Mrs. Hill had to come in and give us fruit buns to try to settle us down.

By the time I had told that story, the soup was hot and we were all starving.

We ate fruitcake and shortbread with the soup and after the soup as well. When Charles was putting things away he found some mince pies in the pantry so we sampled those.

Then Naomi told me about the night that Charles came to collect me from the *Carpathia*. First she asked if it was all right to talk about it. Mostly I hate it when people talk about the disaster, but it was all right, from her. Already she feels like family.

"I wanted to come with him to the dock," she said. "I had never met you, but I just wanted to hug you and take you home, safe and sound, dry and warm and alive. But Charles said that you would not be in any shape to meet new people and that he needed to get you home to Halifax as fast as possible."

She said that Charles was beside himself with worry when all that confusing news first hit, but strong and level-headed and absolutely sure that I would survive.

"That's when I fell in love with him," she said. "For months I had been dithering. I just didn't know how I felt about him. I'm only twenty, after all. But that's when I realized that he's the person I want on my lifeboat with me."

"So I have you to thank," said Charles to me and mussed my hair.

Lifeboat.

Life.

Boat.

This made me cry and that made Naomi cry. Charles took out his big white handkerchief, but he didn't know which one of us to give it to and that made Naomi laugh and that made me laugh and then Charles just looked confused, so he made cocoa instead of trying to understand us. After that there were more mince pies and more talk of the *Titanic*.

That's what we were doing when the parents came home. Mother said that I should be in bed already, but she didn't say it with much gusto.

But now I am in bed and I have one big iceberg-sized thought. All these months I have been saying to myself, "It's over. It's over. It's over." But that hasn't worked. Now I think it didn't work because it isn't over. The *Titanic* sank. Because of that, a young woman named Naomi fell in love with a young man named Charles. And for everybody who was on that ship, whether they lived or died, it's the same. Things happened because of the disaster and things keep on happening. Most of the things were terrible. Some of them are wonderful.

It isn't over. It won't *ever* be over. I am a girl who survived the *Titanic*. That's part of me.

December 21

Last night I slept the whole night through. No dreams. No waking up to check that my shoes were right beside my bed. I didn't wake up until Mother came in. She saw Borden snuggled up to me and just lifted her eyebrows, but didn't say a word.

Today we're going sledding.

This journal is almost full. There is just enough room for me to write about the angel if I squish the writing a bit. What happened last night was frabjous. Like in the poem *Jabberwocky* by Mr. Lewis Carroll.

> *O frabjous day! Callooh! Callay!*
> *He chortled in his joy.*

The frabjousness started over dinner. Charles and I were telling Naomi about our grandparents and all the things we did in England on our trips to see them. For example, both of us went on an expedition to see the White Horse of Uffington, which is a huge outline picture of a horse cut into a hillside. Under the grass is chalk, so the outline of the horse is white. Ancient as can be. Father said to Charles that at least they hadn't taken us to see the Cerne Abbas Giant, and then they both gave that man-to-man laugh and Mother gave a little warning cough that means "drop the subject." They think I don't know that the Cerne Abbas Giant is another outline picture, of a naked man. The grandparents didn't take us to see it, but Grandmother told me all about it. Naomi said that she hoped she could meet Grandfather and Grandmother one day because they sound lovely.

Then, much later when I was asleep, there was a soft knock on my door. It was Naomi. She said that she and Charles had a plan to celebrate the winter solstice and if I wanted to be part of it I should get dressed. But I needed to be quiet. She said I should wear my warm sledding clothes. Of course I wanted to be part of it! She helped me get ready and when we got to the back door, there was Charles holding two brooms, a roll of twine and the turkey platter. He looked like a man with a big secret. I saw by the kitchen clock that it was 2 o'clock!

We slipped out the door and headed along the street toward the Citadel. There was new snow everywhere and our footprints were the first. It was like we were the first people in the world.

Naomi told me the plan. She said it was her idea and all because of the White Horse of Uffington. Naomi and Charles didn't seem like serious grownups, fiancée and fiancé, but just like friends.

When we got to Citadel Hill it was a perfect blank page of snow. Charles tied one broom onto my right arm and the other onto Naomi's left arm. Then, with her carrying the turkey platter, we tiptoed our way right to the middle of the field of snow. We lay down close, side by side, with our heads on the platter. It was cozy. Then we swished our broom arms in giant arcs, back and forth, until we had brushed away the snow right down to the grass. Then we untied the brooms and tied them to our outer legs. This was hard because we had to take our gloves off and our fingers were cold and clumsy. But we managed and then we swished our legs just like our arms. Then we untied the brooms again, pushed the platter down into the snow and then picked it up, scrambled to our feet and tiptoed back to the edge of the field, sweeping away our footsteps behind us as we went.

We didn't look up until we got back to Charles. Then we did.

There she was, the giant mysterious snow angel. We just stood there, hand in hand in hand, admiring her.

"What will they think in the morning," said Naomi, "when they go by?"

"She will become a legend," said Charles. "I'll come as soon as it's light and take a photograph."

"She's the Angel of Citadel Hill," said Naomi.

I thought of the confirmation class where Rev. Hill made Phoebe cry. "No, not angel. She's the Seraph of Citadel Hill."

"Perfect," said Charles. "A secret early Christmas present for all of Halifax."

Then, wet and cold, we hurried home in the moonlight.

There are two more lines left in this journal. I want to fill it up.

Angels from the realms of glory.
Wing your flight o'er all the earth.

ABBY ROBERTS

ALL FALL DOWN
THE LANDSLIDE DIARY OF
ABBY ROBERTS

Frank, District of Alberta
June 1902 – June 1903

BY JEAN LITTLE

Against all odds, Abby and her family survived one of Canada's worst natural disasters, a massive landslide that sent half a mountain tumbling onto their town. But her little brother with Down Syndrome has not fared so well, and her friend Bird isn't in town, so Abby is having a lonely lead-up to Christmas. Then a suggestion from an old friend from Montreal sends her on a new and intriguing path.

The Real Blessings

Friday, December 15, 1905

Today I went to visit Miss Radcliffe. She is house-bound after recovering from a fall. Forgetting how strong the wind can blow in Frank in the winter, she stepped outside yesterday and was bowled over by a sudden, powerful gust. Mother was there but not close enough to catch her before she hit the ground. Mother did manage to lift her back onto her feet, but her face had struck a boulder, she was badly shaken and she had sprained her right wrist.

When I first saw Miss Radcliffe this afternoon, I was shocked at how battered she looked. Her arm was bandaged, her forehead was bruised and her cheek had a nasty scrape. But she scoffed when I gasped. She's not young but she is tough.

"Do me a favour and ignore my war wounds, Abby," she said. Then, before I could catch my breath and say how sorry I was, she demanded to know whether I was still writing in my diary.

I didn't want to talk about it, but her catching me off guard that way made me blurt out that I had stopped writing when Davy was sick, and somehow, in those weeks, it got lost and I couldn't begin a new one afterwards.

She was quiet for a moment and then she said, "I thought that was probably what happened."

The way she said this and the way she looked at me made me squirm. I still don't understand why I felt guilty about not starting to write again. But I did. And I felt angry at her for asking me about it so abruptly. I wanted to tell her it was none of her business, but I couldn't be rude to Miss Radcliffe.

I was trying to think of a way to change the subject when she patted my hand, saying that she understands why I gave up, but that I must go back and write down all that has happened to me in the past few weeks.

"If you think back, Abby," she said, "you will remember how it has helped you to write about your pain before."

"I can't," I started, but before I could say more, she reached into her bag, drew out this lovely notebook and put it on my lap.

"When one is about to begin working on a challenging piece of writing, one needs a new notebook," she told me with a smile that made me lower my hackles. She reminded me that she had always believed I was a gifted writer, and how much she loved reading my work.

I blushed. Then I looked down at the notebook and I could feel the cold, empty place inside me shrink ever so slightly. The first one she gave me, long ago when we lived in Montreal and Father had just died in an accident, did help me get through that confusing time. None of us knew what was going to happen to us — moving to Frank to live in a hotel with an uncle and aunt we had never met, sharing our living space with lots of other people, having to pitch in at the hotel and learn a new way of life. Davy had won people's hearts in no time — well, except people who only saw a handicapped little boy — but Olivia and John certainly found the move difficult at first.

After getting over the shock of the landslide that buried so much of Frank, at least some things improved, like the mines reopening. And Olivia's wedding to Jeremiah cheered us all up. But now I am having to bear this new loneliness, which has been inside me ever since I realized I was going to lose Davy. I have done my best to hide my heartache. Mother guessed, I know, because she felt it too. But the others all believed I had gotten over grieving and was feeling fine. Some people actually said his death must be a relief to me, since he was so disabled and I had always been the one who looked after him.

Miss Radcliffe knew better. She had guessed we

needed her help, I think, because the Slide had left all of us grieving. I cannot explain how she made such a difference by coming out to visit us and then deciding she would move out west to stay. Once she came, she helped me with the high school subjects I did by correspondence, but then when Davy got pneumonia, I had to put my studies aside to nurse him. The doctor had told us he might not survive, so I had warning, but it was still terrible.

Like me, Miss Radcliffe has loved Davy from the day he was born. So when she gave me this notebook, I could not stay mad at her. I knew, deep down, that she was right. So I promised I would try. And it is absolutely true that a new notebook does make you want to start writing. I have begun and I will go on tomorrow even though some of it will be hard to put down on paper.

That is enough for tonight.

Saturday, December 16, 1905

It has been such a strange year. First came all the excitement of Alberta becoming an official province. I have never before attended so many big parties, helped put on concerts, marched in parades, attended picnics or heard so many politicians and ministers and other bigwigs make endless speeches. I hate sitting still listening to men going on and on about what a fine place we live in, what a grand future we are about to begin, how we must all work together to make wonderful progress come about. All the words sound the same, all the messages preachy and tedious.

When I am seated on a hard chair, being bored to death but trying to look impressed, struggling to keep from yawning, I wonder if all the other people are having as much trouble not twitching as I am. My feet wiggle, the back of my neck itches and I feel as though I am about to let out a shriek.

Olivia has no such trouble controlling her body. She sits there, looking saintly, with her hands clasped in her lap and her eyes gazing at the pontificating personage as though she is deeply impressed. (Miss Radcliffe will like that bit.) But I know that my sister is not really listening the way she seems to be. She is planning what she will cook for Jeremiah's supper, concocting programs for her piano pupils, deciding what her next dress pattern will look like and delighting in thoughts about her precious baby Frank (christened John Frank — John for his uncle and Frank for the town, but everyone calls him Frank). Olivia is dear to me, of course, but her appearance of perfection can be downright irksome.

What is the matter with me? This diary is supposed to be filled with the stories of my life and it is sounding stuffy instead. Is it because I keep thinking of Davy and nothing seems funny or lively now? I keep reliving the last days. It was terrible listening to him fighting to get a breath. It was as though he was drowning. When he finally gave up, I was glad in spite of wanting to keep him with me. Nobody, especially a little boy, should have to suffer like that.

The last word he spoke before he lost consciousness was my name. He was in my arms and he opened his eyes and looked up at me and said, "Aa-bee." I felt as though he had reached out to pat my hand one last time.

I was still supporting him when he stopped breathing. The silence that falls at that moment is louder than any sound.

I hate it when people tell us that his death was a blessing and that he has gone to a better place and that his suffering is over. He only suffered at the very end. He was a truly happy person. And his *life* was a blessing, not his death. When people say he is in a better place now, I try not to let my rage show and I nod my head without speaking. If I opened my mouth to tell people my thoughts, they would be shocked.

Nobody living in our hotel says his death was a blessing. Every one of them loved him. I am not the only one who misses him.

That is enough for now. I am going to bed.

Sunday, December 17, 1905

In the night, after I had started writing in my diary, I made up my mind to write a cheerful poem to give Miss Radcliffe for Christmas. And I have started it! It is going to take me a while to finish, but I'll put down the start here now.

I am going to write it out on good paper to give to her. She said I should write something that would give my thoughts a fresh direction. And I have. Miss Radcliffe is the one person who believes I will become a writer. It was thinking of her that made me begin my poem with the wind.

My Alberta

Knock-down winds and big, blue sky,
That's my Alberta.
Snow-capped mountains, proud and high,
That's my Alberta.
Prairie dogs and antelope,
Wildflowers blooming on a slope,
Folks who never give up hope,
That's my Alberta.

A place with sunshine at its heart,
That's my Alberta.
A Province in a rush to start,
That's my Alberta.
The prairie stretching mile on mile,
Hills where you can dream a while,
Friendly faces, quick to smile,
That's my Alberta.

I think she will really like it if I can keep going. I really like it myself. I do feel happier.

Perhaps tonight I will fall asleep without missing Davy's body curled up next to mine.

Monday, December 18, 1905

I made up more verses this morning before I got out of bed. I am proud of them. I rewrote them this afternoon while I did chores. It was fun, and it helped to take my mind off missing Davy, too. Here they are.

The way the mountains hide the sun,
That's my Alberta,
Before the afternoon is done,
That's my Alberta.
Watching wildlife wing and prowl,
The mountain elk and snowy owl,
And hearing the coyotes howl,
That's my Alberta.

The echoes when somebody calls,
That's my Alberta.
Booming back from canyon walls,
That's my Alberta.
Blazing stars that light the night,
Eagles poised upon a height,
Then soaring in majestic flight,
That's my Alberta.

Olivia was here with her baby this morning. Frank is so sweet, even though he does drool sometimes. My sister is an excellent parent. Mother beams at Olivia when she is rocking Frank and singing silly songs she makes up. I wonder if she ever thought of writing a poem.

Here's more of mine.

> *A place with space to spread my wings,*
> *That's my Alberta.*
> *Lullabies my sister sings,*
> *That's my Alberta.*
> *Waking glad for each new day,*
> *Watching grasses dip and sway,*
> *Knowing here is where I'll stay,*
> *That's my Alberta.*
>
> *Prairie paths I love to roam,*
> *That's my Alberta.*
> *This country where my heart's at home,*
> *That's my Alberta,*
> *The Canada where I belong,*
> *Where I will grow up proud and strong,*
> *And which I'll love my whole life long,*
> *That's my Alberta.*

It has rough spots, but Miss Radcliffe won't mind. Maybe I should not have put Olivia in, but it rhymes so perfectly. And I like it. I will show it to Mother tomorrow.

Wednesday, December 20, 1905

I not only miss Davy, I also wish my friend Bird had not left Frank when school let out. But tonight I have a new friend. She seems to have heard me wanting her and has come to comfort me. I was lying awake listening to the little noises you hear in the night in a hotel. People cough sometimes or shut the door to the bathroom or drop something.

I was thinking about my poem when all at once I heard someone crying. Whimpering is a better word maybe. I waited for the sound to stop, but it didn't. It was so sad and small and it seemed to be right at the back door, just outside my bedroom. Finally I couldn't bear it and I pulled on my robe and tiptoed out and stood at the door, listening. It got louder. It was so forlorn. That is the exact word. Miss Radcliffe would be proud of me for coming up with it.

I opened the door and in she tumbled! She's a puppy. She's very young, but her eyes are open. She's still fluffy with baby fur. And she looked up at me and threw back her little head and positively wailed.

I picked her up and she was shivering. The pads on her tiny feet were freezing cold. She keeps nipping at my fingers. Her tiny teeth are incredibly sharp. I think she has mistaken me for her mother. She surely needs a mother — her bones are sticking out. I can't see how she stayed alive out in the snow. I am calling her Scruffy at the moment, but I will have to think up a better name. I will not name her Alberta. She is too small for such a big name.

I gave her some milk to lick off my finger. Tomorrow I'll find a bottle — that will work better. I have brought her inside my room and tucked her into Davy's spot. She got enough milk that she has fallen asleep. I cannot believe I have a puppy. I have never had a pet. Father did not approve of them. I didn't need one while I had my Davy, but now she seems just what I was needing without knowing it.

Thursday, December 21, 1905

I just have time to scribble in the next bit of my Alberta poem while the puppy is having a nap. It is just one verse but I like it.

Rattlesnakes and rodeos,
That's my Alberta,
The cottonwood, the prairie rose,
That's my Alberta.
Riding up a rocky trail,
Hearing the train whistle wail,
Finding friends who never fail,
That's my Alberta.

Later

Scruffy is now Scrap. Nobody has any idea where she came from — like me! Nobody knows where I came from either. But I was adopted by the most loving of mothers. I will try to be Scrap's adopted, most loving mother.

Cousin Mark named her. John said we should call her Cannibal after she tried to eat his thumb, but Mark said, "How can you mind a bite from such a scrap?" Then Jeremiah invited her to chomp on his wooden leg. She tried, but did not find it to her liking. She backed up, sat down and sneezed mightily. Then she pretended we were not laughing at her. It was so funny.

I was a little worried Mother would say we did not need a puppy, but she didn't.

I have been kept busy the last few days because of doing schoolwork, helping with the work of the hotel and looking after my puppy, who is always howling that she is hungry. I could say *whimpering*, but it is such a loud noise that it won't do.

Davy would be enchanted with her. One of his best friends was Mark's dog Dulcey, before she was killed by the Slide.

I think my poem is done, although it is hard to stop.

Christmas is almost here. Mother loved my poem. She found me some paper that rolls up into a sort of scroll to write it out on. Scrap does not approve of my writing, though, so I will have to wait for her to go to sleep. Otherwise she leaps on the pen as though it's her worst enemy.

I wish Bird had not gone back to live with her family. She would like the poem, I know. I'll keep a copy and she can read it when she visits. Bird is the "friend without fail" in the poem, of course.

Sunday, December 24, 1905

It is Christmas Eve. I was going to take the poem over to Miss Radcliffe's, but it turns out Mother has arranged for John to fetch her in the wagon tonight so she can spend Christmas with us at the hotel. I am going to try to wait to give it to her in the morning, although that will be hard. I admit I am very proud of it.

Monday, December 25, 1905

Christmas Day. Scrap got me up early, wanting to open her present. I got her a red collar and a bowl that says *DOG* on the side of it. I also got her a rubber ball to chase. Mark was in Lethbridge and went to a store and got her a rubbery little bone to chew on. She adores it even though her baby teeth are so tiny. She is a darling.

Olivia brought little Frank over for the day, and it is lovely to watch the two little ones romping with each other. Scrap bit Frank but Frank bit Scrap, and neither of them seemed to mind.

Miss Radcliffe loved her poem. She said I must work on it some more and then submit it to the paper.

She thinks people in Frank will all be asking for copies. She also suggested that I make up a special verse about Frank, maybe mentioning the Slide and how we are rebuilding.

"Once a teacher, always a teacher," Mother said. Then she told me I was lucky, and she is right.

> *A puppy by the name of Scrap,*
> *That's my Alberta.*
> *Who just fits curled up on my lap,*
> *That's my Alberta.*
> *My mother and my family,*
> *As close as any four could be,*
> *Singing round the Christmas tree,*
> *That's my Alberta.*

> *Miss Radcliffe who will read this rhyme*
> *Here in Alberta,*
> *And share my joy this Christmastime,*
> *She's my Alberta.*
> *I'm running out of words to write*
> *But I am filled with deep delight*
> *Knowing my world is growing bright,*
> *Here in Alberta.*

I know that it's not as good as the other verses. But it's like eating peanuts. You think of another rhyme and you are into it again.

I did not tell about the book Mark got me. It is

called *The Shuttle*. It is by Frances Hodgson Burnett. It was written for adults and he got it for me! I think it is a love story.

I blushed when he gave it to me and he laughed. He does not seem to be going out with a girl now that Nancy has moved away and got married to somebody in Lethbridge. I liked her, but she was not good enough for Mark.

Bedtime, Christmas night

When I came to bed, I found Mother waiting in my room with a last present. It is so lovely. She had an artist who often comes to the hotel paint a picture of Davy. He started it before Davy grew ill, so it shows a happy little boy smiling his funny smile. It's a miniature, but it looks so clear and beautiful.

I had not said how terribly I was missing Davy throughout the day, but of course Mother knew. The painting is on the table, out of Scrap's reach, but where I can see it whenever I look that way.

Now I will shut my eyes, but I can't resist writing down once more how much Miss Radcliffe loved her poem. Her face shone. She has already been after me to start polishing it. She said, "I told you writing would help you heal, Abby." She did and she was right.

I thought this first Christmas without Davy was

going to be miserable, but I was wrong. Writing about him brought him back to me somehow. He is still with me. And now I can just turn my head to smile at him.

Goodnight, Scrap. Good night, Davy. Good night, Alberta.

Mary Kobayashi

Torn Apart
The Internment
Diary of Mary Kobayashi

Vancouver, British Columbia
May 1941 – January 1943

By Susan Aihoshi

In the aftermath of Japan's bombing of Pearl Harbor on December 7, 1941, Mary's family and all Japanese Canadians living within 320 kilometres of British Columbia's west coast were forced to leave their homes. Their possessions and businesses were confiscated, and they were shipped to hastily constructed internment camps in the B.C. interior, to endure a brutal winter in crude living conditions. A year later their circumstances have improved, but Mary faces new challenges. Perhaps writing to her friend Sachi will help.

Dear Sachi

Dear Sachi,

Arigatō for your last newsy letter! I'm sorry I haven't written you lately. I miss you so much, especially now when I'm experiencing a real *conundrum!* (I'm trying to impress Emma as well as Sister Agnes by expanding my vocabulary.) I wish you were here to talk it over. Do you remember how much it helped sharing our thoughts back in Vancouver? I hate that we're so far apart and in different camps. It's been over a year since I've seen you! But I hope that by writing this down as if you were really here, things will get better. I'll write every few days and send this scribbler to you when my problem gets solved — if it ever does!

Speaking of letters, Tad has written again. He wants us all to come east and join him in Toronto. He says there's more opportunity for us, and he even thinks most people in the city are getting used to Japanese Canadians. Mama doesn't believe him! I wonder if what Tad really means is that the non-Japanese tolerate us, like they do here in New Denver. Sure, we go into the village stores to shop for things we can't make or grow ourselves. We go to their churches, and some of us even work for them. But all the time we keep to ourselves, go to our own schools, have our own gatherings and live separate lives.

Sachi, I don't have a single *hakujin* friend here like Maggie or Ellen, even though we live in the main part of the village now. I know you said that in Lemon Creek, except for a few high school teachers and government officials, everyone there is Japanese Canadian. So maybe what happened here last week would never have happened in *your* camp.

Last Friday as Nora and I were walking in the village, we noticed a big commotion in the field beside Bob's Ice Cream Parlour. Two groups of boys had gathered, one made up of kids from The Orchard and the other of village kids. To my dismay, I spotted Harry in the middle, arguing with a village boy around his own age. Harry was shouting that he wasn't a liar, while the other boy kept insisting that he was. Then he called Harry "a lying Jap!"

I was horrified hearing those words, but I was even more upset when Harry tried to hit the boy, who was a lot bigger! Who knows what would have happened next, but Bob came outside and shouted at everyone to leave before he called Corporal Sayers. He said the uproar was ruining business!

I grabbed Harry's arm and marched him home. You can imagine how relieved I was that a big fight didn't break out or that the RCMP weren't involved. When I walked into our house still clutching Harry's arm, Mama stopped sewing and wanted to know what happened.

Harry claimed it wasn't his fault. That boy simply wouldn't believe his description of Woodward's escalators. The boy has never even been to Vancouver, but he insisted Harry was lying about the store having stairs that move! Mama asked why Harry was talking about Woodward's in the first place. It turns out that the other boy was bragging about seeing all the big shops in Nelson. So of course, Harry just *had* to tell him about Woodward's.

Mama sighed and told Harry he was grounded. And then she said I have to pick up Harry from school every day until Christmas, to keep him out of trouble! So I can't help Nora and the other high school kids plan our Christmas party. And then yesterday while I was getting Harry, his teacher asked if I would help her kids practise *their* Christmas play. Two nights a week! Because Miss Miyaki is Kay and Emma's friend, I couldn't really refuse. Aren't you glad you don't have a little brother!

But that still isn't what's really bothering me,

Sachi. Before I went in to help Miss Miyaki, I noticed a little boy crying outside the Grades One and Two cabin. I've never seen any child look so unhappy. He looked *inconsolable!* When I went over to see what was wrong, he ran away. Harry told me the boy is Stephen Takada. What could possibly be making him so sad?

Sunday, December 12

Hi, Sachi,

Papa brought home some of last week's Vancouver newspapers from the drugstore yesterday. I know you wrote that you don't see the papers very often, which may be just as well. They had a lot of stories about the second anniversary of the bombing of Pearl Harbor. That certainly stirred up more anti-Japanese feeling, judging from the letters. Isn't it bad enough that our families were broken up and we had to leave our homes to move here? That poor Geechan died when he was sent away to work at a road camp? That you and I spent weeks without knowing where our fathers were before they were allowed to rejoin us? We barely survived last year's terrible, terrible winter. And people still want us out of the province entirely. We're not even Japanese, for heaven's sake, we're *Canadians!*

Most of the village shops have put up their Christmas decorations. It's strange to be thinking of Christmas when we're all still so far from our real homes. Harry's mention of Woodward's reminded me of our old life. December in the Slocan Valley sure isn't like being in Vancouver! Ever since I arrived here, I feel as if I'm in the middle of a strange dream. I look around and can see how beautiful it is right beside Slocan Lake, surrounded by mountains. And yet we had no choice in coming here. Yes, we have running water and electricity at last, but we still have so many restrictions. Rationing is one thing, because everyone has to do it. But doesn't it make you mad that only Japanese Canadians have to carry identity cards all the time? I guess you and I will have to get one when we turn sixteen. Remember how we used to bicycle with our gang all the way to Stanley Park and back? Now Papa needs a permit just to take the bus to Kaslo to see Aunt Eiko. And I overheard him say that the Security Commission may soon force Mike to go east, whether he wants to or not. Even if we do go back home when the war is over, what will it be like if so many people still hate us so much? It's a real *dilemma*, isn't it?

Tuesday, December 14

Sachi, I thought you might enjoy hearing about what Harry is up to now. His class is doing a play based on the Christmas Day chapter of Dickens's *Pickwick Papers*. I haven't read that book, have you? Miss Miyaki wants to "expand the children's horizons" beyond *A Christmas Carol*. Harry's been cast as Mr. Nathaniel Winkle, who is always bragging about his *proficiency* in various sports, only to demonstrate his complete *ineptitude*. Mrs. Yamasaki's daughter Dori plays Arabella Allen, who ends up marrying Mr. Winkle! I wonder whether Harry and Dori might get married when they're older.

In the play, Mr. Winkle pretends he's an expert at ice skating. When Arabella asks him to demonstrate, Mr. Winkle *demurs* and says he has no skates. Because he wants a pair himself this Christmas, Harry delivers that line with particular *panache*. But skates are found, which Winkle reluctantly dons and promptly falls down. It's amusing how Harry must become *adept* at being *inept*!

I didn't see Stephen Takada when we left The Orchard today. After supper, I asked Papa if he knew the Takada family, since he knows so many people who visit the drugstore here. Mr. and Mrs. Takada used to live in Vancouver like us, but in Kitsilano. They were both born in Canada and Stephen is their only child. They live in one of The Orchard cabins, close to the lake. Papa was going to say something else, but Kay dropped in unexpectedly, so I'll let you know what he tells me later.

48

Dear Sachi,

I finally discovered why Stephen cries. It's not a nice story. Now I'm *really* upset! I was helping Miss Miyaki again after school today and the kids were being really *rambunctious.* She finally decided to give everyone a short break and asked me to take half the children outside for a few minutes while she calmed the others down, inside.

When I got my group outside, I spotted poor Stephen behind one of the other cabins, surrounded by half a dozen boys. They were circling him, all the while making barking and howling sounds. Stephen stood stiffly in the middle, looking completely miserable as tears streamed down his face. Sachi, I was shocked, even more than when I heard that village boy call Harry a Jap! I told the kids under my charge to stay where they were while I ran over to help Stephen.

But as soon as they saw me, those naughty boys ran away faster than you can imagine and so did Stephen! I must have looked furious when I returned, because the kids from Harry's class went quietly back inside without my saying a word. I scarcely remember what happened after that because all I could think about was that Stephen's tormentors were kids just like him! And why were they barking at him like animals?

Dear Sachi,

I've been down in the dumps lately, so I'm writing you again. I've already told you about those boys tormenting Stephen, which made me both sad and angry. It's even worse than I thought. Harry and I were in The Orchard this morning helping Mrs. Yamasaki and her daughters to bake cookies for the school pageant. Like you said, everyone's been saving up sugar for weeks. I asked Bonnie, who's in Grade One with Stephen, if she knew why those boys pick on him. She told me that Stephen doesn't speak Japanese. They think it's funny that someone who looks so Japanese can't understand a word of it.

Then tonight Papa finally finished what he was going to tell me the other day. When he was at the bathhouse last week, some of the men were discussing *inu*. When I asked why were they talking about dogs, he explained that the word is actually a terrible insult — it means traitor! And then Papa said a few people call Stephen's father that because he believes Japan is going to lose the war. So when those boys barked at Stephen like dogs, they were really insulting his father! Isn't that mean? Even if Stephen doesn't understand what they're saying, he knows it's something awful.

What's wrong with thinking that Japan is going to lose the war, Sachi? Isn't Japan our enemy? Of course

I'm worried for anyone who still has family there, but I'm just as worried for Canadian soldiers — men like our old neighbour Danny Franklin — and their families.

Did I tell you Tad is still trying to enlist? I hate this war. I thought I'd left bullies like Billy Foster behind in Vancouver. It's horrid that Japanese Canadian kids are being cruel to each other! Sachi, do you remember that part of our Girl Guide pledge, to be useful and to help others? Here's my chance! I'll help Stephen somehow.

Sunday, December 19

Dear Sachi,

I'm still down in the dumps, even after church. I miss Geechan and Tad. You must think about Oxford Street often, like I do. I wonder whether we had a good crop of fruit from our backyard trees this year. There was no one to harvest it, so maybe it all went to waste. Harry's been busy making construction-paper garlands. Part of me hopes we'll have a tree here this year, and part of me just wants to celebrate back in our old home.

As we get closer to Christmas Day, I still feel *ambivalent* about being here. Like you, I was glad to be able to attend high school this fall. But what will it mean when we graduate? Can I go on to university like Mama and Papa want me to, or will I have to take any old job to make ends meet? I can't sew like Mama and Kay, and I'm certainly not as brainy as Emma. She should have been able to become a nurse like she always wanted, but instead we watched how all the Japanese Canadian student nurses in Vancouver were fired after Pearl Harbor. What kind of work will Papa and Mama have if we go east? I'm sorry to sound so negative, Sachi, but it's difficult thinking about the future when we have so little control over our own lives.

At least Mike has taken matters into his own hands. He announced his New Year's resolution today — he's joining Tad in Toronto as soon as possible in January. He was tired of having the Security Commission dictate what jobs he can have and how much money he makes. He wants a real job with real prospects.

How does your family feel about moving east? Do they want to stay here until the war is over, and then try to go back home? Or do they want to go east to the great unknown? The thought of having to move again frightens me.

Monday, December 20

Dear Sachi,

I'm in a much better mood tonight. Somehow you and Maggie must have read my mind. When I went to the post office today, there were cheery letters from both of you! I hope your high school pageant is a success, although it will be over by the time you read this. And I'm so glad you did well on your exams. I know you've been especially worried about Math, so it must be a relief to discover you got good marks. I should hear what my results are soon. Sister Agnes is always telling me to work hard and I'll be rewarded. I hope she's right!

Tuesday, December 21

Dear Sachi,

I was so busy today! The full rehearsal for the elementary school's Christmas program took place at Bosun Hall this afternoon. Everything went off without a hitch. I didn't see Stephen after it was over, so I hope he's been able to avoid those *yancha* boys. Here at home, Harry keeps practising falling down as Mr. Winkler. He's driving me crazy!

A big parcel arrived for us in the mail from Tad. It was full of smaller packages, one for each of us. Harry's convinced that his will be ice skates. I hope he won't be disappointed! I wonder what's inside mine.

And tonight Mike brought us over a little fir tree! We spent all evening decorating it. Harry's garlands were put to good use and we made several *origami* ornaments from old newspapers. Mama miraculously found a few strands of tinsel in one of our old trunks. The tree looks lovely and really cheered me up. I'm starting to feel like Christmas, in spite of everything.

Thursday, December 23

Dear Sachi,

So much happened today, it's a challenge to get it all down for you! I'm writing this wrapped in a blanket, sitting beside the kitchen stove. Although I'm completely dry now and wearing flannel pajamas, I'm still chilled from my unexpected dip in the lake. Corporal Sayers just left our house. Such excitement! Where shall I begin?

This afternoon everyone in the family went down to a packed Bosun Hall for the pageant. Almost everyone in our community was there. Stephen was sitting with his parents when we arrived. He looked as sad as ever, but at least he wasn't crying. Somehow all the classes kept to their allotted time, probably thanks to Emma's organization. I watched Stephen trying to hide himself in the back row when his group got up to sing "Santa Claus Is Coming to Town." It's hard to believe that some of those cute kids could be so mean.

I confess I lost track of Stephen once Harry's class put on its play. Harry's role as Mr. Winkle was the hit of the entire show! When all the children finished their various performances, everyone sang "God Save the King." Then the mothers brought out their baking and there were masses of people milling around, chatting and eating. I saw the Takadas but Stephen wasn't with them and I thought nothing of it. Maybe I should have, in *retrospect*!

Harry ate too many cookies and began racing around. I worried he'd get a swelled head from all the compliments he received! Mama asked me to take him outside to burn off his energy. That's when Mike said he had to drop off a load of old wood down by the Sanitorium, so he suggested I walk Harry there. He'd pick us up and drive us home later. "Capital idea!" said Harry, repeating one of his lines, and the two of us headed south.

The beach in front of the hospital was deserted. Harry raced to the water, his feet clattering on the stones. Suddenly he stopped and said, "What's that noise?" We heard splashing coming from a corner of the bay. "Over there!" he shouted.

The two of us ran to the shore. I saw a dark shape in the water. Stephen was hanging on for dear life to a piece of wood, thrashing about to keep from tipping over!

I shouted at Harry to run to the San for help. Then without thinking, I kicked off my shoes, threw off my coat and ran into the lake. The water isn't that deep until you're farther out, but it was sooooooooo cold! I knew that Stephen wouldn't be able to hang on much longer, so I took a deep breath, plunged in and swam towards him as fast as I could. He was just about to go under when I reached him.

Sachi, it was so hard keeping his head above water! And I was so cold! I *had* to get back to the shore fast before one of us gave out. By this time, Harry had returned with Dr. Uchida and Mr. Mori. And Mike showed up too, thank heavens! Mike and Mr. Mori both ran right into the lake. Just as I was about to sink, Mike grabbed me and Mr. Mori grabbed Stephen. They carried us onto the beach, where Dr. Uchida was waiting with some blankets.

I was cold in the water but even colder once I was out! My teeth wouldn't stop chattering. Stephen's lips were blue and he kept coughing up water. Before I knew what had happened, we were wrapped in those scratchy grey Commission blankets and brought into the San.

Even though I was still cold, I was fine otherwise. Stephen had swallowed a lot of water and was in worse shape. The nurses put him in a spare bed and packed hot water bottles around him. Dr. Uchida phoned the RCMP and asked someone to fetch Stephen's parents.

Sachi, I'm so proud of Harry! He stayed at Stephen's bedside until the Takadas arrived. They'd been running around the hall searching for their son ever since the pageant ended and were worried sick. Harry refused to leave the San until Stephen finally fell asleep, exhausted. Mike drove us home. Corporal Sayers stopped by to tell us Stephen will likely be fine after a good night's sleep. That's what I'm doing now — going to bed!

Dear Sachi,

News travels fast here! At school today, everyone had heard how I rescued Stephen. I was embarrassed by the attention, so thank goodness our Christmas party distracted everyone.

And what a surprise that was. Nora and our classmates had transformed the dining room with homemade decorations. The sisters had prepared us a feast! There were candles on the long table and favours at each place. The centrepiece was a splendid cake that Sister Agnes said was a Christmas tradition from the nuns' home in Québec, a *bûche de Noël* or yule log. Father Clement said a short prayer before we ate some of the most delicious food I've ever eaten. Afterwards, we sang Christmas carols.

Sachi, I had such a feeling of happiness that I haven't felt in a long time. I was hoping hard that same feeling would somehow reach Stephen too.

And my wish came true! When I got home, Mama said that Harry went to see Stephen. He was much better today, so Dr. Uchida let his parents bring him home for Christmas. When Harry returned, he announced he was tired of being the youngest in this family. He's offered to be a big brother to Stephen! Not only is Harry going to keep an eye on Stephen after school so those kids won't pick on him, but he's going to teach Stephen some Japanese words. That should be interesting! Isn't it great that Stephen has someone to look out for him now? My *conundrum* is solved!

December 25, Christmas Day

Dear Sachi,

I hope your Christmas was as good as mine! That happiness I felt yesterday continued today. This morning our family went to mass, and St. Anthony's was full of our friends and neighbours. During Father Clement's sermon, I thought of how Mary and Joseph had travelled so far and were looking for a safe place to rest that long-ago Christmas. No one wanted them. And yet everything worked out somehow. My New Year's resolution is to be more positive!

Then we walked home and opened Tad's presents. Harry *did* get his ice skates! Mama got a big box of chocolates, a real treat during rationing. And Tad gave me my first fountain pen. I can't wait to use it! I'll mail you this scribbler next week, Sachi, so you can read about my adventures. I can't wait for your next *dispatch*.

Thanks for "listening" and have a very happy New Year!

As always,
Mary

Rosie Dunn

A Country of Our Own
The Confederation
Diary of Rosie Dunn

Ottawa, Province of Canada
April 1866 – July 1867

By Karleen Bradford

The country of Canada is more than one year old now. Christmas will see Rosie much busier than usual, if Cook has anything to do with it. And though Rosie is settled in her role as a servant, she thinks the scatterbrained nursemaid who is tending little Jonathan is making a mess of it. Then another situation comes to light which draws Rosie's attention in a way she never would have expected, and she has no idea how she might help.

❦

A Candle for Christmas

Monday, December 14th, 1868
Ottawa, Dominion of Canada

We are in our fine new stone house now and, although it is a sight warmer than the dreadful old wooden house that we lived in when we first came to Ottawa, it is in the usual Christmas turmoil. Not helped at all by that ninny of a new nursemaid, Beth. Sure, I cannot see why Missus Bradley ever hired her. Mind you, Beth is all sweetness and light when she is around, but Cook and I know the truth of it. Beth is the most scatterbrained mooncalf I have ever met. I have heard of people who don't have the wit to boil water, but until I met Beth, I never believed it to be true. The trouble is, she is fond of baby Jonathan and he loves her, and that's all Missus Bradley sees. She doesn't see the carelessness.

How can I tell her? She would just reprimand me and say it isn't my place to criticize her choice of nursemaid, and of course she's right. 'Tis a worry, though.

Tuesday, December 15th, 1868

Spent the day running errands and going to the shops for Cook. She is deep into the preparations for Christmas. Mister and Missus Forrester will be coming as usual, so Bessie will be here to help out again. I'm looking forward to seeing her, as it's been awhile since we have been able to get together. Not that we'll have much time to visit and catch up with each other's news, though.

Cook is calling. She needs help in the kitchen. Not much time for anything but Christmas at the moment, actually.

Later

That Beth is beyond useless. I had just finished helping Cook with some last-minute puddings — she always fears that there will never be enough food when, truth be told, there is already enough to feed half of Ottawa — when Briney turned up with the daily delivery of the water barrels. He had a day off from his job at the mill and was helping out because his da is not doing too well. There was a new fellow working with him, and that daft Beth seemed very taken with him. Flighty, she was, and making calves' eyes at him. Meanwhile, poor little Jonathan was toddling around unsupervised and I caught him just before he stumbled into the hearth.

I let out a screech and was pleased to see her jump

a mile. What did she do then but grab the poor child out of my arms and glare at me as if I were the one at fault. I caught Briney's eye over her shoulder and he raised his eyebrows at me. He has heard me complain about her often enough; now he has seen for himself how neglectful she is. Briney's new helper, Jack, didn't notice anything amiss, and just kept mooning at Beth as if he had taken leave of his senses. If he had any senses in the first place, that is.

I saw a woman by the courthouse this morning when I was passing by. I don't exactly know why, but she caught my attention. She was carrying a small bundle. She looked up at me for a moment as we crossed each other's paths, and I was brought to a standstill by her eyes — the saddest eyes I have ever seen. I wonder who she is and where she was going.

Friday, December 18th, 1868

Thank goodness we got some snow last week and it has covered up the frozen mud. Not so slippery for walking about. It looks much nicer, too. White and pure instead of dirty brown. Briney and Jean-Louis took advantage of it to go into the woods across the river and cut down a Christmas tree for us. I do thank Queen Victoria and Prince Albert for introducing this German custom — I love it!

We will not bring the tree in and decorate it until Christmas Eve, of course, but Cook and I are busy making decorations for it. Jean-Louis brought a barrel of cranberries again and Cook and I made her delicious cranberry sauce, but we saved enough berries to make garlands for the tree. I have been busy stringing them.

Cook made the sweetest little cookies in the shape of stars. We will hang them, as well as popcorn balls, which I will make tomorrow, and we'll string bright ribbons around the tree to make it look as festive as possible.

Missus Bradley even has some pretty little ornaments that she will put on, with a star for the very top. Then Mister Bradley will fasten the candles onto the branches. They will only be lit on Christmas Eve for a short time, because of the danger of fire, but they will make the tree look lovely.

I have also been secretly making gifts to put on the tree for the family. I made:

—a pen wiper for Mister Bradley, as he is always staining his cuffs with ink

—a needle case for Missus Bradley, with a rose embroidered on it (I hope she will recognize it as a rose, which is her favourite flower, as I am not all that handy with a needle)

—a pincushion for Beth, in hopes that she will organize herself a bit

—a rag doll for Jonathan, who does love soft toys

I could not think of what to get Briney or Jean-Louis, so I made them each a special cake. I must admit I made Briney's a bit more special.

I did not make a gift for James. Even though he condescends to treat me more politely now that I am no longer suspected of stealing that bracelet, he still obviously dislikes me. I suppose a good Christian would overlook that and find some little treat for him, but I will not. I know that he would receive whatever I gave him with a sneer and would probably toss it in the trash heap. If that makes me a poor Christian, so be it. I will confess it next Sunday and not trouble myself over it. I do not see that much of him, anyway, as he is always off attending to Mister Bradley and driving him around.

I sent off a package to my own family earlier on this month. I made a toy for Timothy as well, and sweets for Paddy and Bridget. I sent tobacco for Da and a scarf for Mam. Missus Bradley gave me some of her own fine, soft wool to make it. She is such a kind lady. Then I made mittens for Mary Margaret and a wee quilt for her little Rosie. Named after me!

My family's package of gifts for me arrived last week, but the best gift I have ever received was my big sister naming her babe after me.

Saturday, December 19th, 1868

I saw that same woman today near the courthouse. Everyone on the street was in a bustle and greeting everyone else with cries of "Merry Christmas!" and "Good Cheer to you!" but she just made her way along the street with her head down, still clutching a bundle, and not taking any notice of anyone. Her whole being looked so dejected and hopeless. I could not help it — I followed her. She went through a little door into the jail at the side of the courthouse. What could she have been doing there?

Monday, December 21st, 1868

I have found out who the woman is, and it is such a sad story. I was running errands for Cook, as usual, and passed by the courthouse again. There was the same woman, trudging along with her bundle, bent over against the wind. Without thinking, I went over and offered to carry her bundle for her. She looked startled, then clutched it closer and shook her head.

"No!" she said. It was almost a cry. "No! I must do this myself!" Then she scurried into the building.

A man — a guard, I think— was standing at the door. When he saw me there, looking confused, he told me what the story is. It seems the poor woman is the wife of Patrick James Whelan, the man who was convicted of the shooting of Thomas D'Arcy McGee last April. The newspaper was full of it at the time, and the talk around Ottawa was of nothing else. It seems Mister Whelan is said to be a Fenian, one of the Irish who hate England and all the British, and considered Mister McGee to be a traitor to Ireland for helping our prime minister achieve Confederation. The belief is that that's why Mister Whelan shot him, but the guard told me that Mister Whelan steadfastly maintained his innocence at the trial and maintains it still. Nevertheless, he is to be hanged. The woman who visits him is his wife, Bridget, who brings him his luncheon every day.

The hanging will be some time in February. It is to be done in public at the Carleton County Jail right here in Ottawa. Briney says he is going to watch. I will not. To see a fellow human being die, whether he is guilty or not — I could not bear it.

It is so sad. I cannot imagine what Missus Whelan must feel like. And Mister Whelan — what a terrible fate he faces! I know myself what it feels like to be falsely accused of something, even just stealing a bracelet, which was bad enough. But what would it be like to be accused of *murder* if you didn't do it? And to be *hanged!* How can they bear the waiting, knowing what is going to happen and knowing there is nothing they can do about it?

Wednesday, December 23rd, 1868

Beth has done it now. I am still trembling with fear. This is what happened.

I was sent out for some last-minute shopping and Beth asked Missus Bradley, as the weather was not too cold and it was not snowing, if she could take Jonathan along on his little sled for some fresh air. It seemed odd to me, as Beth is not one for walking if she can avoid it and she is always complaining about the cold. She usually prefers to sit in the nursery and let Jonathan amuse himself with his toys at her feet.

We had just gotten to Sparks Street when Jack, that new fellow who works with Briney's da, appeared. He made such an elaborate pretense of being surprised by the meeting that I knew at once he had been waiting for us. No wonder Beth had been anxious to get out.

He took over pulling the sled with Jonathan on it and soon he and Beth were well ahead of me. I tried to keep up, but I had to stop into Bate's grocery store for tea. When I came out, they were a piece ahead of me on the other side of the street. Just as I caught sight of them, Jonathan spied me and called out to me. I had promised him that he could look in the shop windows that were all decorated for Christmas, and I could see that Beth was hurrying him past them and paying no attention to him whatsoever. I started to cross over when, to my horror, I saw Jonathan slide out of the sled and start to toddle toward me. Beth never even noticed.

I cried out, but at that exact moment a cart came careening by, pulled by two horses that looked to be almost out of control. I have never moved so fast in my life. I dashed across the street, almost under the hooves of the horses, and reached Jonathan just as he was about to step in front of them. I threw myself at him and we both landed in the snow beside the street. A lady walking by screamed and several other people cried out. The man driving the cart let out an oath and finally managed to get the horses under control.

Jonathan shrieked and I pulled myself off him. I was so afraid that I had hurt him, but he was all right, just terrified. I looked up to see Beth staring down at me.

Can you believe what she said? "Please, Rosie. Don't tell Missus Bradley! Don't tell on me!"

I snatched the straps of the sled out of her hands and bundled Jonathan back into it. I patted him and soothed him and promised him that we would look into every store window on the street. Gradually he calmed down and I brought him home, Beth scurrying along behind me, begging me to be silent about the accident all the time. I just ignored her. Jack conveniently disappeared.

When we arrived home, Missus Bradley was waiting for us. A friend of hers was waiting with her.

Beth's begging was all in vain, as Missus Bradley's friend had seen what happened and had already told her the whole story.

Beth was dismissed forthwith.

But I cannot stop shaking.

Thursday, December 24th, 1868
Christmas Eve

The house is fast asleep and I am beyond tired, but I must write down what a lovely evening it was.

Briney and Jean-Louis brought the tree in after dinner at noon today, and we set about decorating it and putting our presents on it. Brutus, silly dog that he is, took far too much interest in sniffing at it, but Mister Bradley soon put a stop to that. Then Brutus lay down and kept looking at the tree in a confused sort of way. I think that lack-wit dog thought we had brought it in for his personal use. My little Sophie is much more clever. She just stalked around the tree disdainfully, then sat down with her back to it and started grooming herself. It was obvious that she did not think the house was any place for a tree. She was almost sitting on Brutus's tail, but he pretended not to notice. He learned long ago, after many a scratched nose, not to trifle with Sophie, no matter that she is only about as big as his head.

I gave Jean-Louis and Briney their cakes. Jean-Louis gave me the sweetest little cat that he had whittled out of wood. It looks just like Sophie. He is still so shy, though, that Briney practically had to force him to hand it over. Then Briney gave me his present. It took me aback. It was a ring! A slim band decorated with blue enamelled forget-me-nots. I didn't know what to say, but just stammered out some kind of thank you. I am wearing it now and looking at it on my finger in the candlelight as I write. It gleams and sparkles.

Who would ever have thought that Briney would give me such a pretty thing? He must have saved some of his wages for months to afford it.

When we had the tree all decorated, we had a small supper, then the Bradleys went to their church and I went to Mass. By the time we all came home it was dark and very cold, but a light snow was falling and everything looked quite beautiful in the light of the gas lamps along the street.

We returned to the house and Mister Bradley lit the candles. Then we all exchanged presents. I think they liked the ones I had chosen for them. Jonathan was barely awake, but he clutched the rag doll I had made for him and snuggled his face down into it. Missus Bradley gave me a lovely, warm shawl. I shall treasure it.

We sat for a while in the dark room, enjoying the silence and the flickering light from the candles on the tree. Then, from the street outside, came the sound of carolling. Missus Bradley opened the door to the carollers, and I made haste to warm up some cider for them.

Friday, December 25th, 1868
Christmas Day

A very different day today. It was hustle and bustle from the time I woke up. Cook nearly ran me off my feet. But the Christmas dinner was excellent and Missus Forrester made a great show of complimenting Cook on her dishes. Cook was so pleased she puffed up like a partridge.

Bessie and I did not have a moment of free time, but we still managed to catch up with each other's news.

One thing happened that could have been very embarrassing, but ended up just being amusing. I was preparing the table for the dinner when I happened to glance at the tree. Something seemed odd about it. I went over and peered more closely at it, then jumped back, startled, when I saw two bright little eyes staring back at me from deep within the branches. It was Sophie! She had curled herself up on a branch, right in the middle of the tree, up against the trunk.

I reached in and tried to get her out, but accidentally dislodged some of the decorations and one of Missus Bradley's precious glass ornaments nearly fell.

I drew back, wondering what I should do. Another attempt to get the cat out was just as unsuccessful. Then I heard Cook calling to me and I gave up. I left Sophie there, and there she stayed for the rest of the afternoon. I had a difficult time keeping a straight face when Missus Forrester complimented the Bradleys on the lovely decorations on the tree, though. If only she knew one of them was a live cat! Fortunately, when it came time to light the candles again, Sophie had taken herself off and disappeared back up to my room. I said a little prayer of gratitude.

The Forresters have gone now. I put Jonathan down for a nap, and I finally have a moment to sit down and rest.

No, I haven't. Missus Bradley is calling me.

Later

I hardly know how to write down the news I have just received.

Missus Bradley was in the parlour and, when I went in, she told me to sit down. I was astonished, as that has never happened before. Then she told me that she has decided on a new nursemaid for Jonathan. My heart sank. I knew this was necessary, but I have loved having the care of him since Beth left. Then she asked me if I would like to know the name of the new nursemaid. I was a mite confused, but I nodded.

"Her name is Rosie," she said.

"Like mine?" I blurted out, stupidly.

"Not *like* yours, Rosie. It *is* your name. Mister Bradley and I have decided that you are old enough now, and no one could care for Jonathan better than you. You are the new nursemaid."

For a moment I could not answer. Then I blurted out again, even more stupidly, "Truly?"

"Truly," she answered with a smile.

No more blacking the stove. No more boiling the laundry. No more scrubbing the kitchen floor on my hands and knees. No more running to Cook's beck and call.

I am no longer a kitchen servant. I am Jonathan's nursemaid.

Monday, December 28th, 1868

Today was a bright, sunny day, with the snow sparkling and crisp. Not too cold, so I dressed Jonathan up and took him out for some fresh air.

We walked by the courthouse and, sure enough, there was Missus Whelan with her bundle. I had not been able to keep from imagining what *her* Christmas was like while everyone else was celebrating the season and rejoicing with family and friends, and I had a secret plan in mind. I approached her again, but this time I did not offer to carry her bundle.

Instead, I held out a small package of my own to

her. "Please take this," I said. Before she could say anything, I spun Jonathan around on his sled and hurried off.

It was one of the candles from our tree. Missus Bradley gave it to me on Christmas Day. I had been wanting so badly to be able to do something for poor Missus Whelan, but could think of nothing that was within my power, nothing that could possibly lessen her worry and grief during this dreadful time. Then I thought of how the candles on our tree had brightened up our gloomy parlour and made a haven of warmth and brightness within it, and I thought of giving my candle to her.

Such a tiny thing.

But perhaps, just perhaps, it might bring a small spark of light and comfort to a grieving woman and her husband.

Jane Browning

Exiles from the War
The War Guests Diary of Charlotte Mary Twiss

Guelph, Ontario
June 1940 – June 1941

By Jean Little

When Charlotte's family agreed to take in war guests because England was being bombed by Germany, they didn't know Jane Browning and her brother Sam would be staying so long, or that the war would still be going on, over a year later. But it is, and Jane has settled in so much she decides that she'll start keeping a diary like Charlotte's. She's even become sort of an older sister to Pixie, a war guest who came to Canada along with her and Sam.

The Rescuers

Sunday, November 15, 1942

Ten days ago, on Guy Fawkes' Day, I turned eleven. I told Charlotte that I wanted a diary like hers for my present and she ordered one from the bookstore. She had to wait to get one like hers, but today she gave it to me. It is perfect. I hope I will like keeping a diary as much as she does. I have never done it before.

I got lots of lovely presents on my actual birthday, but I will only tell about a few.

Sam gave me a really fat box of crayons with lots of colours you don't usually get, and a colouring book with pictures from fairy tales. I really like it. Sometimes I change the pictures. I turn princesses into beggar girls dressed in rags, for instance, and make up stories about them while I colour. Sometimes I put in a cat or draw a big cloud in the sky. Colouring is a lot more fun when you do it my way.

Eleanor gave me a copy of *Jane of Lantern Hill*. I love it. I have read it once and I'm starting again.

George sent Charlotte money, all the way from England, and she bought me two Nancy Drew mysteries. I don't like them nearly as much as *Jane*, but we pass them around at school. It is nice to have some to lend.

I feel sorry for a couple of the girls whose families never get them books. Grace Allen stole one. At recess, she ran down the stairs to the toilet with it in her hand and, when she came out, she didn't have it any longer. She had hidden it in her underpants! Later, when she had to go up to the board, you could see the shape of it under her skirt. The others picked on her, but I kept out of it. I don't like her either, but Charlotte says I must be nice to her because her family is really poor.

Grandpa gave me a Dr. U.B. Well bag. It looks like a real doctor's bag, even though it is made of cardboard, and it has a toy stethoscope in it and candy pills and a thing to look into ears and a chart to check people's eyesight and tongue depressors and a toy needle to give shots. There's a thermometer too, although it doesn't work.

Pixie loves playing hospital with me when she comes over from her aunt's. She was here for my birthday supper — Mum invited her because she came over from England with me and Sam. She wanted to start playing hospital as soon as I opened the kit. But Mum said not when we had guests.

"What guests?" Pixie asked, looking around.

"Sam and Robbie," Mum told her with a smile.

"They aren't *guests*," Pixie said, tossing her head. "They're just boys."

Everybody laughed.

I can't go on writing. My hand is tired and so are my thoughts.

Monday, November 16, 1942

The birthday present that really surprised me was the china cat Charlotte's Aunt Carrie gave me. She told me she has had it for years. She said he looks like "that cat of yours."

She was right. I showed the china cat to Only, but he just glanced at it and stalked off. Aunt Carrie said my darling cat certainly lives up to his full name, The One and Only.

I got a doll from Mummy and Father in England. Mummy had made her an extra dress out of an old one of mine she found. She told us about clothes rationing and how they are supposed to make do and mend instead of buying new things. She made our brother William a shirt out of an old pillowcase. She said it looks funny but he is too little to mind. I think we will be sending William an outfit from Canada one of these days.

The box from England came three days early, but I made myself wait. I opened it the moment I woke up on my birthday. The wrapping paper smelled like home and made me lonesome. In the wrappings there was some newspaper, telling about what damage was done by bombs. I wish I hadn't read it. It scares me, thinking about my parents maybe being in danger.

Nearly bedtime

I wonder if I should start with saying that I'm Jane Browning and my brother Sam and I were sent to Canada as War Guests to save us from the bombing in England. Sam was sent to the Bennetts, who live across the street from the Twiss family, who got me.

At first, I didn't know what to call Charlotte's mother and father, but I call my real parents Mummy and Father, so we decided I should call the Twisses Mum and Dad.

Dr. Twiss is a professor and Mrs. Twiss teaches school. She quit teaching when she got married because back then married women weren't allowed to teach. But now so many men who were teachers have gone overseas to fight the war, they need the women to come back. She really likes teaching, so she is happy about this.

I guess I've barely mentioned Charlotte's older sister Eleanor. I like her a lot. She's almost as old as George. We met him when we first came, but we didn't get to know him very well before he enlisted.

I did like him though. He gave me run-unders on their swing.

Charlotte turned fourteen last June. I really love her. She seems like my real sister.

Tuesday, November 17, 1942

Even though I don't know George that well, I think that Mum and Dad are worried about him right now. I am not sure why. He almost died when his ship was torpedoed, but he and his friend Bertie and some others got in a lifeboat. It drifted around in the Atlantic Ocean for days. Everybody thought he had drowned. But they came ashore and, even though he was in the hospital for ages and has a crippled hand, he is getting better now.

But something is making Mum and Dad unhappy. They used to share George's letters and laugh about them, but not lately.

Friday, November 20, 1942

I asked Dad if George was coming home to Canada soon. He said he didn't know. He looked so miserable when he said this.

I felt nosy but I wanted to know more, so I asked if he was well now.

"The wounded spirit takes time to heal," Dad said. Then he went into the front room and closed the door.

George has met my parents. Mummy and Father

visited him in the hospital and then later he went to our house for tea. He was the one who told us that Mummy was going to have a baby. It was a great shock! But I guess it helped prepare us for the news when William was born.

I have seen his picture, of course, but I do wish I could meet the real little boy.

We got a letter from England yesterday, and Mummy said that she and William may be evacuated even though the Blitz is over. She did not say much about it, but Dad told us their letters would be censored in case they let slip something to the enemy. I don't think Mummy would know anything the enemy would care about. Reading her words makes me homesick.

I am tired of writing in this diary. I think I won't keep it up. Yet, when I look back, I like reading about what has happened to me since I got it.

Tuesday, November 24, 1942

I had an earache last night so Mum kept me home from school. It stopped hurting and I got to stay in bed and listen to the radio. After I heard "The Happy Gang," I finished reading *Jane of Lantern Hill* over again. Jane's grandmother is as mean as the witch in *Hansel and Gretel.* I like it that Jane lives in Ontario some of the time instead of always in Prince Edward Island.

Pixie is coming over tomorrow so we can play with my doctor kit. I have decided that one of my dolls will have a heart attack. And my new one from England will have a broken leg or arm. I like bandaging them and making them wear slings.

Wednesday, November 25, 1942

Something terrible happened today. I can hardly believe it even yet. Pixie says it was an accident, but somehow she let my new doll, who I named Elizabeth Rose after the princesses, fall out the bedroom window. The poor darling, who came all the way from England without a scratch, crashed to the ground and broke. She is not exactly shattered, but the top came off of her head and her eyes rolled back out of sight and one of her arms is smashed.

I was crying my eyes out when Aunt Carrie came by. She told me to gather up all the pieces carefully and put them into a bag she had. She's going to take E.R. to The Doll Hospital when she goes to Toronto next week. I did not know there was such a place in the world.

I wish I could go too, but Aunt Carrie will be busy. Then she said maybe I could come when she picks E.R. up.

Mum told us tonight that we are all going on the train to see the Santa Claus Parade in Toronto. After the parade, we will go to see the Eaton's windows, which are specially decorated for Christmas. We might even go to Toyland to choose a present.

In England we don't have Santa Claus. Well, maybe it is the same, but we call ours Father Christmas. He doesn't come with a sleigh and reindeer, but he visits each house. You put your stocking on the foot of your bed.

Charlotte said it would be perfect if the doll was ready on the Santa Claus Parade day. Then we could all go to The Doll Hospital. Aunt Carrie laughed and said, "We'll see," just like Mum does.

Mummy says the same thing when we want her to promise us something. She says it is because once in a while you have to break a promise, and so it is better to wait and see.

Wednesday, December 2, 1942, night

I was right about my not liking to keep a diary as much as Charlotte does. My life just isn't exciting enough. But going to Eaton's Toyland to see Santa Claus himself does sound exciting, even though I do like Father Christmas better than this Santa person. I suppose they are the same, but they don't sound like it to me. Well, Santa Claus is an American. There is Saint Nicholas too and Kris Kringle. Mum says they all stand for the spirit of giving. I like the animals they have. Santa has all those reindeer, and Saint Nicholas, who is in Holland, rides a big white horse.

Pixie wanted to come to Toronto with us and she begged and pleaded. When Aunt Carrie said, "No," Pixie flopped down on her knees, clasped her hands together, rolled her eyes up and tried again. But Aunt Carrie declared she wasn't up to taking someone so flighty and full of highjinks. Pixie sniffled a bit but gave up. Even she can tell when Aunt Carrie turns into a stone wall.

I know what Aunt Carrie meant about her being flighty though. She's seven but she acts as though she is five. She's always losing things or getting the giggles or bursting into tears. Or letting other people's dolls fall out of windows. Yesterday she was fiddling with a necklace of Mum's and let it slip out of her hand and down the heat register. She doesn't know I saw.

When she had gone, I tried to fish it out, but I couldn't quite reach down far enough. I won't tattle, but I hope someone gets it before Mum misses it. She likes that necklace a lot.

Friday, December 4, 1942, after school

We are having a Christmas concert at school. Our class is singing "The Campbells Are Coming" and Sam's class is singing "Do You Ken John Peel?" They are very English songs. The school choir is doing "Land of Hope and Glory." Sam and I knew them before we came here. At least it is better than having to sing "There'll Always Be an England," the way we had to when we first came here. We did get sick of it.

I think we should sing "The Maple Leaf Forever" and maybe "Alouette."

Mum got me a dress that has a plaid top, to wear for the song about the Campbells. It is serge and a bit scratchy, but it does look Scottish.

I feel tired tonight and not in a writing mood. I feel sort of sick, too, but I hope I'm not, not this close to the concert.

Saturday, December 5, 1942

Here's some real news for you, diary.

When I woke up this morning, I felt as though I really was sick, but I didn't tell because Pixie was coming over this morning. She arrived just after lunch, but she was not her usual self. I was trying to figure out what was making her so grumpy, when she burst out crying. I went to push her hair back and before I even looked at her forehead, I could feel she was burning hot. She moaned out something about her eyes hurting.

So I called Mum and she felt Pixie's forehead and looked worried. She sat down and lifted Pixie up onto her lap. Then she unbuttoned her blouse and said, "Oh, no!"

I ran to look and Pixie had grown all blotchy. Her eyes were red and the blotches were all over her chest and even inside her mouth. There were a couple hidden under her bangs. She has the red measles!

Mum telephoned Pixie's aunt. She said she had wondered about Pixie's spots because her older boy had measles. Mum looked furious, although she didn't let it sound in her voice. She thought P. was going to infect Sam and me, but Sam had the red measles back home in England, and the Twiss children have all had them.

Not me, though. And I was hot, too, and feeling sicker every minute.

While Mum was busy with Pixie, I went into the bathroom and looked at my chest and there were spots. They aren't as bad as Pixie's. I went and had a drink of water and waited a few minutes while Mum was talking to Pixie's aunt. Then I checked again just to make sure. The spots were there and I was pretty sure there were a few new ones.

I was on my way to show Mum when I heard her wail, "If only Jane doesn't get them."

I almost hid in our bedroom, but I had to tell. I unbuttoned my top buttons and went and stood in front of her and waited. It took her a moment to notice. When she did, she buried her face in her hands and moaned. Then she grabbed me and gave me a big hug.

"Oh, Jane, my poor darling," she said. "To bed with you. I suppose this means we'll keep Pixie here too. Her aunt was hinting that she wanted me to offer.

I didn't because of you, Jane. But that poor woman has those two rapscallion boys to look after."

So, diary, I have the red measles and we won't be going to Toronto after all. Our house has a quarantine sign on the door. Aunt Carrie will bring my repaired doll home when she's fixed, and we'll visit The Doll Hospital the next time Pixie sends a doll flying.

Oh, I do feel sick. My eyes see everything through a blurry fog, and they hurt when I try to read. I am having trouble writing in this journal too. Mum says it won't last. I am so hot and miserable. I am giving up keeping this journal until I'm well again.

Friday, December 11, 1942

I'm feeling much better. Pixie is a lot sicker than I am. They have called the doctor to come three times. She keeps crying out and what she says doesn't make sense. Mum sits by her bed and wipes her forehead with a cold cloth and gets her to sip ginger ale. I am not exactly jealous, but I do feel a tiny bit neglected.

Dad read to me tonight. I got to choose, so I picked the one about Bre'r Rabbit because it always makes him laugh. But it didn't tonight. He hardly ever laughs these days. He didn't even quite finish it. He said he was sorry and kissed me goodnight and went downstairs. I am sure it has something to do with George. I wish I knew how to make Dad happy.

Goodbye for now.

Tuesday, December 15, 1942

I am well enough to start writing in you again, diary. I have to tell what has happened.

I woke up last night because I heard somebody tiptoe past my bedroom door. Then I heard Mum telling the person to hush. And she sounded as though she was having a hard time to keep from bursting out laughing, or maybe crying.

I got up and crept out into the hall. They didn't see me. But I saw them.

It was *George* who was making her laugh. This morning I found out that George is home on leave! He walked in and surprised them.

Last night, I scuttled back to bed. I don't know George very well except from hearing stories about him. I'll write more tomorrow.

I feel way better now that George is home and everyone will cheer up.

Pixie is still sick, although I don't think she is in danger of dying any longer.

I heard Mum tell Robbie's mother that they had been afraid for her when her temperature went up to 105 degrees.

Thursday, December 17, 1942

George has not been discharged from the Navy, even though he was wounded. He's going back to work in an office now instead of on a ship. He is home on leave, and the Twiss family is overjoyed to have him back in Canada.

He is extremely thin and he looks terribly tired. Eleanor and Charlotte keep teasing him and trying to cheer him up, and he smiles at them, but the smiles don't reach his eyes. He hardly talks. He made Mum laugh that first night, but I have not heard him laugh since. Christmas is coming, though. Surely everyone will be joyful at Christmas.

He keeps his bad hand hidden in his pocket all the time and never speaks about it. He only uses his good hand, never the wounded one. He gets Mum to cut up his food before we sit down to eat.

I can't talk to him about any of this. George is nice, but it is as though he is speaking to us from behind a glass wall.

Just one more week till Christmas.

Friday, December 18, 1942

Last night I was in bed but not asleep yet when I got to thinking about Grandpa. He is jolly and good at making jokes. He has what my mum calls a "rollicking laugh." He also has one eye that turns in all the time, but it doesn't bother him at all. He was born that way.

When we were staying with them in Coventry, before we came to Canada, a lady visitor asked him, all of a sudden, "Wouldn't you be more comfortable if you wore dark glasses? Then nobody would see your eye."

She made me angry saying this, but Grandpa just laughed one of his big laughs.

"You mean *you'd* be more comfortable, Dinah," he said. "My crossed eye doesn't bother me one bit."

She went red and started stuttering and then everybody was laughing. But I think that is how George should be about his hand. I can't explain what I mean, but Grandpa forgets how his eye looks until somebody says something, and then he turns it into a joke.

Of course, Grandpa wasn't wounded. Maybe that makes a difference. It would be harder to laugh about a wound.

I loved it when that lady went red. Grandpa was right about *her* being the uncomfortable one.

I miss him. I like the Twisses, but I do sometimes long to be with my own family back in England. Sam does too. We don't talk about it in front of Pixie, because she was so little when we left England that we think she is forgetting.

Sunday, December 20, 1942

I know some more facts now and I understand things better. Charlotte explained. George had to have his hand amputated. He has a metal hook instead of a hand. He got an infection that wouldn't heal, and then something called gangrene, and they had to cut his hand off.

I remember reading about gangrene in a book about Florence Nightingale.

No wonder he keeps it hidden away and is so sad.

Monday, December 21, 1942

Pixie has cheered up even though she is not all well. My rash has long gone and I can see clearly again. What a relief!

Mum says having George at home will make Christmas a day to celebrate in a way we haven't since before the war. He smiles at her. But it is such a tired smile, not a bit joyful. I can't watch or I get a lump in my throat.

Tuesday, December 22, 1942

Dear Diary, just wait until you hear what happened last night! Pixie and I worked a miracle. Really.

She had gone up to bed and I thought she was sleeping. So I tiptoed when I went up so I would not wake her. I heard George's voice saying, "It's time you went to sleep, chicken."

I peeked through the door, which was slightly ajar, and I saw George sitting in Mum's big rocking chair with Pixie curled up on his lap.

I was starting to creep away when I heard her ask to see his hook.

I was horrified because I knew she must have upset him. He didn't answer. I strained my ears, but nobody spoke. So I stayed still and waited.

Then Pixie gave a joyful squeak. "Oh, George, that is super!" she said. "It feels so strong. Like Captain Hook's in *Peter Pan*. Does it bend?"

George laughed at her. It was a croaky laugh, but still a laugh.

Then she burst out, "You have to show Jane. I'll get her."

I was about to run away fast when George said, "No, Pixie. Jane wouldn't like seeing it. You don't mind because you're a child, but it would make Jane sick to have to look at it."

Well, I knew that was wrong. He shouldn't be thinking that. I would *not* be sick. So I marched straight into the room. And I said, "Jane *does* want to see it. Jane has been wanting to look at it ever since she found out you had it."

He was dumbfounded. But he had not had time to hide it. I moved fast and took a giant step. Then I reached out and grabbed hold of his hook.

And then, Diary, I was inspired. I told George I thought he could do Pixie a big favour. I explained how I'd seen her playing with Mum's necklace when it slipped out of her hand and went into the heat register, and she couldn't get it out. And that when she wasn't around, I tried to get it, but I couldn't, either. "But you *could* do it, George. Your hook could reach."

For a minute I thought he was not even going to try. Then Pixie leaped off his knee, shrieking with delight.

"Oh, please, George," she begged. And she caught up his hand, the real one, and pulled him over to the register.

He had not said a word, but he went down on his knees, slid his hook through the grating, hooked the chain and slowly fished up the necklace. He almost lost it once, but managed to catch it again. Then he held it out, dangling on the hook, so Pixie could take it.

Good old Pixie scooped the chain off his hook and went dancing around the room singing.

George and I looked at each other and grinned.

Then Mum came in and there was his hook, out where we could all see it. He almost shoved it out of sight, but then he didn't

"Look!" Pixie shouted. "He's got the best hook in the world! And he rescued your necklace."

Since then, George has come back from wherever he was hiding himself along with his hook. He is going to take us to see *The Mark of Zorro* during the holidays.

And tonight when Sam was standing on the step-ladder trying to put the star onto the top of the tree and the ladder started to teeter, George jumped to

steady it and he used both his hand *and* his hook —
cool as a cucumber. (Well, a cucumber wouldn't be
able to help, but George was so matter-of-fact. He
didn't seem to notice.)

And I know, because I saw them, that Eleanor has
got me figure skates like the kind Barbara Ann Scott
wears, and I bet she'll teach me to do figure eights and
other fancy twirls the way she does herself.

Dad met me in the hall when I was going to bed
and he kissed me on top of my head.

"Well done, Jane," he said.

"What did I do?" I asked him. I really wasn't sure
what he meant.

"You healed my boy," he said, very softly.

Ever since he said it, I keep smiling like that
Cheshire Cat in *Alice in Wonderland*. Because you
know what, Diary? It's not just George that Pixie and
I helped. It's Dad. He keeps smiling now too. Just like
the rest of us.

Rose Rabinowitz

Pieces of the Past
The Holocaust Diary of Rose Rabinowitz

Winnipeg, Manitoba
January 1948 – April 1948

By Carol Matas

The only survivor of her family, Rose was forced first into the Warsaw Ghetto and then into hiding in the forests and countryside of Poland. She has begun to settle into her fourth home since immigrating to Winnipeg after World War II, and is becoming closer to her friend, Susan. Susan's parents, Eva and David, are welcoming, as are Susan's four brothers. But making the transition to a safe place is not always simple.

The Light and the Dark

Sunday, November 14, 1948

This is not at all what I thought would happen!
Now what do I do?

Let me start at the beginning, as the last few days
have been so hectic. And, dear diary, I also want
to say an official "hello!" I have put away my other
diary forever, but discovered I missed writing. When
I mentioned that to Susan, well, suddenly you, dear
diary, appeared out of nowhere on my bedside table.
I knew right away you came from Eva, and when I
thanked her she didn't deny it.

While I was in such a grateful mood Eva sprang
something on both me and Susan. She told us we
should try out for the Christmas pageant at school.
This surprised me for two reasons. Firstly, we are
Jewish. Why would she want us to participate in a
Christmas pageant? Secondly, Eva has never demanded anything of me, anything at all, so why this?

I asked her. That must have been last Wednesday. Eva explained to me that both Susan and I need to try to make more friends. She said she was happy we had found each other, but that now we needed to expand! Well, of course I have my friends from the old country here — the other orphans — and I see them every Sunday. In fact, I just returned from seeing Oskar and Jakub and the rest of them at the downtown YMHA. As usual, we swam, played ping-pong, talked and caught up on the week. Actually, I think this was really about Susan making more friends, not me. But since we are now inseparable, I can understand why I was included.

The auditions were set for last Thursday. Susan and I talked about it and we agreed to go ahead because Susan assured me we would never get chosen anyway, and we had nothing to lose — and at least her mother would be happy that we tried.

We went into the auditorium together. There were lots of girls there and we were all given a seat on the folding chairs set up in rows, and then we were called up one by one to read from the script. We each read the part of Mary. Mr. Snider told us that based on our reading, we would be assigned different roles, like townspeople or sheep or something. Each of us had to sing. Susan had the entire group almost in tears when she sang "Silent Night."

I did too, but for a different reason! I could see the

other students wincing as I sang, and some couldn't stop themselves from giggling. For once I didn't blame them.

When it was over I told Susan that she would definitely get a role in the choir, and then I forgot about it all. Until Friday, that is, when everyone who auditioned was called to the auditorium again and Mr. Snider announced right off the bat that I would be playing the part of Jesus's mother, Mary! I thought I would faint dead away! Oh, and Susan was to be the lead singer in the choir! I should have said no to being Mary right then, but I was so shocked!

That night at Shabbos dinner Susan told the family what had happened. They were all so excited and congratulated me. When four big strong loud boys heft you on their shoulders in the middle of dinner, it is quite the experience! After that I didn't feel I could tell them that I felt strange about being in a Christian play. They didn't seem to think it was strange at all, but I suppose they grew up with Christmas pageants and have always taken part in them.

After dinner that night we played charades and Saturday we went to synagogue and then in the afternoon to a movie, *The Best Years of Our Lives*, and of course I was busy all day today, so Susan and I didn't get to talk about it until after supper tonight.

I asked her if it isn't somehow against our religion. She shrugged. "It's just a tradition. A Christmas concert is an important event, and maybe Jewish people feel more accepted when they are in it than if we all refused to participate."

"I asked Oskar," I said. "He says I shouldn't be afraid to say no if it makes me feel funny." I thought about it for a minute. "The truth is, your whole family is so excited, Eva especially, I don't want to let them down."

Susan sighed and then admitted that she felt exactly the same as I did, but that she couldn't — for the life of her — think of a good enough reason to say no.

Monday, November 15, 1948

There is a new royal baby. It is all anyone is talking about, although David said it was silly in comparison to Prime Minister Mackenzie King stepping down after so long as PM, and a new prime minister, Louis St. Laurent, taking his place. Eva said the royal baby was much more interesting to everyone, and I think she is right. We're waiting to hear what he will be named. At school it was all the talk, because he will be the future king.

We had our first pageant rehearsal today during Math class! This is a benefit I didn't see. Most rehearsals will be in school hours, so we get to miss class. I suppose that might also have been a consideration when the teachers chose the students. I am well ahead of my class now in most subjects — unlike when I first arrived — and have even caught up in Math. And I suppose my accent must be pretty much gone or they certainly would not have given me the part.

Friday, November 19, 1948

A busy week, both with rehearsal and school work. At first I was excited because I could miss classes, but I can't miss the work, so I have to do it at home. Susan and I are doing twice — no, *three* times — the amount of homework now, which is why I haven't had a chance to write in your pages, diary.

The concert is on December 15. That seems very far away now. The boy playing Joseph is in Grade Seven and seems to have developed a crush on me. He hangs onto my every word and sometimes forgets his lines when he is looking at me! I am at least a head taller than everyone in Grade Nine — maybe why they chose me to play the mother, since I look older. Barry gazes up at me with this adoring look. Susan has started to tease me about it.

The pageant is really very short and is mostly acted without words while the choir sings, so I'm not sure why the pageant players have to be at rehearsal as much as the choir. Maybe next week will be better.

Sunday, November 28, 1948

It seems that all I do in these pages now is explain why I have been writing so little. But this week was even worse than last! More homework and just as much rehearsal, although almost all of it is either sitting around or striking poses while the choir sings. Pageant is right! It is not a play — the words I read for the audition are really the only words I speak. The rest is miming: first so happy when the baby is born, then astonished when the three wise men come, then astonished again when the stars shine, and then the choir keeps singing and I just pose, sitting with my arms around Joseph and the baby. (Which Joseph likes way too much!) And of course the baby Jesus is a doll all wrapped up in a blanket.

At any rate, today I took the bus downtown to the Y to meet up with the other orphans, as usual. After we swam, I talked to Oskar about the pageant. I found myself describing to him the two months in the countryside when I had to pretend to be a young Catholic girl who was living with her aunt — that was hard. In fact my "aunt" was a total stranger who ran her own farm, but who agreed to take me in and protect me from the Nazis. I remember going to church with her. She taught me how to make the sign of the cross, and how to mouth the prayers. My life depended on my acting. If I had done one thing wrong, not only would I have been caught and killed, but so would she.

Perhaps that is why the longer the rehearsals go on, the more the past comes back to me and the worse I feel. When I was living at the farm, Mama was in hiding in the camp with the fighters, without me, and I was so so lonely for her. Not as lonely as now, of course, because then at least I knew she was nearby. Then I knew there was hope that we would be together again.

Now that hope is gone forever. Until death there is always hope. Right up to death. After that — nothing.

Saturday, December 4, 1948

I am not going to apologize again! Oh, maybe I will! But I really have been busy, dear diary, and the only reason I can take time to write today is because a blizzard is about to hit the city. It struck Brandon already and is headed here. We've had a lot of snow and the wind has been bad, so we're hunkering down and staying inside today. No *shul,* no movies, just reading and a promise of playing Monopoly later this afternoon.

I hope the streets will be cleared by tomorrow so I can go to the Y and see Oskar. Since he lives in the north end of the city and I live in the south, it really is the only time we can meet.

Sunday, December 5, 1948

See, dear diary! Two days in a row, no apology needed! But that's because Saturday was just the start of a massive blizzard and we've been stuck inside all weekend and I'm not even sure whether we'll be able to go to school tomorrow. Jonathan beat us all at Monopoly twice in a row.

I've been reading *The Woman in White* all weekend. I had to convince Susan to leave the light on when we went to bed last night. What a scary story! But I like it! I'm going to read *Frankenstein* next. Morris is lending me the books he thinks will scare me the most! Big brothers!

I just called them my brothers. Do you think my real big brother would mind? When we were in the Ghetto, Abe spent his entire life trying to protect me and keep me from being scared. Still, he might be happy that right now I can actually *choose* to be scared.

Thursday, December 9, 1948

It's going down to -22 tonight and -28 on Friday. So Eva is taking me shopping Saturday for a brand new wool coat. I've grown out of the one Rita gave me last winter. Eva says Susan needs a new coat too. This will be the first new coat I've ever had.

Saturday, December 11, 1948

The new coat is black with a white furry collar! And big black shiny buttons. It is the most beautiful thing in the whole world. I actually cried, and Eva pretended she didn't see and so did Susan. And Eva bought me new woollen stockings and new boots with woollen lining in them! And two new dresses and three skirts and two blouses and two sweaters. All my sleeves had been stuck up around my elbows, I have grown so much, and my skirts were way above my knees.

I have folded everything and put it all away neatly and hung up the dresses. I don't know how to thank Eva, but she treats me just like her own daughter, so Susan and I both said thank you and she said we were welcome and that was that. Except I am crying again now.

Sunday, December 12, 1948

The play is in a few days. I asked Oskar and Jakub whether Jews believed in an afterlife and resurrection. Jakub says we believe in a messiah coming one day and some believe in an afterlife, but the emphasis in Judaism is on today, the here and now. In other words, don't wait for the world to come. Do your good deeds now — just in case this is all there is. Not too comforting, but practical.

Speaking of the here and now, my swimming is so good now that I can beat anyone. I tease Jakob and call him old man (at eighteen!) and tell him I'm bound to be faster. Oskar, being only a year older than me, almost fifteen now, has to be gracious in defeat.

Wednesday, December 15, 1948

The snow was so heavy today, we all had to walk to school for the pageant tonight. I was very nervous, but since everyone was depending on me I decided, as we trudged through the snow, that it was way too late to quit, so I'd better do my very, very best. Also, when we arrived, I found Barry shaking in a corner of the stage! He had such terrible stage fright that I had to try to calm him down and convince him he could do it — so I had no *time* to worry about myself. And once on stage it was actually easy! Susan was so wonderful the choir received a standing ovation.

Lots of people came up to me afterwards and shook my hand and told me how excellent I was in my part as Mary. I almost blurted out to each of them, "I'm Jewish, you know!" But I didn't, and anyway, I suspect a lot of them already know I'm Jewish and they don't seem to care that it isn't a Christian playing Mary.

On the walk home, Susan told me she had been invited to Sally's house for lunch next Sunday and to play at Margaret's house next week, so Eva's plan has worked. Susan is worried, I think, that I will mind her having other friends, but I really don't because I have Oskar and the rest of my friends at the Y.

Something else, though, is making me feel strange, but I'm not sure what it is. A feeling that is nagging at me like a dark cloud threatening rain or even lightning and thunder.

Thursday, December 16, 1948

The blizzard is so bad that school has been cancelled and we are staying home today. I'm writing this from the basement. I am in a small room down here — well, not a room, a closet near the furnace — and I am in here with a flashlight. No one knows I'm here.

I woke up early this morning from the worst dream I have ever had in my whole life, and came right down here. I discovered this place when I first examined the house after I moved here last spring. When the family was in bed, the very first night I was here, I went over every inch of the house to see if there were good hiding places in case anyone came to round up the Jews again. I also checked for a good way to escape.

I found this little place and kept it in mind should I ever need it. I know that no one is coming to round up the Jews today. Well, they couldn't if they wanted to, there is so much snow. But I need to be here. Where it is safe and quiet and I am alone, because . . . because last night I dreamed. Last night I was back with Mama, hiding in the cave. She made me stay down there, while she went up and confronted the men hunting us.

It is fitting for me to be somewhere like this, somewhere small and dark. Alone. Why should I be in a lovely bedroom full of new clothes? Why should I be taking bows in a play? Why should I be alive at all?

The last time I was with Mama we were in the cave together. That's where I belong. I can hear people calling my name. But if I call back they will take me out of here and make me live in that happy bright place upstairs. I shouldn't be there. I deserve to be here.

I dreamed about my family last night. Mama and Papa and Abe and Sophie and my aunties and uncles and cousins. Mama and Papa appeared to me just the way they looked after they had been murdered. Eyes with no life in them, just staring . . .

I can hear everyone calling to me. They are worried, I can tell. But I can't move.

I'm thirsty.

It must be night. It's so dark.

I've had another dream.

This one was so different. Papa was shaking me awake from a nightmare and calling my name — *Rozia, Rozia* — and saying that as long as I am alive, my family will live too, in my thoughts, in stories I will tell about them, in my heart. He said, *We are here watching over you. We haven't left you, and I'm going to prove it to you.*

I wonder what he means.

Friday, December 17, 1948, morning

After I wrote that last entry, my flashlight went out and all was dark. I fell asleep. I was awakened by Susan shouting at the top of her lungs. "I found her! She's here!"

And then David was there and he carried me up to my room and Eva made me drink and eat and use the bathroom and take a hot bath. It was 2 a.m. And after I'd had my bath, Susan said to me, "I finally fell asleep. I was so worried, but I fell asleep. And a man came to me in my dreams. He said he was your papa. He said you were hiding in the cellar. He said, *Tell Rozia I will always watch over her.*"

We were in our room alone by then, sitting in our beds and no one else heard this. I stared at her.

"But *I* dreamed of Papa too, and that is what he said — and he said he would prove to me that he was watching over me."

We were both silent for a moment, taking this in. Then Susan asked, "Why did you hide?"

"I don't know," I said.

"You don't need to hide anymore," she said. And she came over to my bed and motioned for me to lie down. I did. She tucked me in just like Mama would have and she said, "You can sleep now."

And then I fell asleep.

And I had another dream. Papa was there. He was lighting the menorah for Chanukah. *A miracle,* he said. *Enough oil for one night and yet it burned for eight days. And our life was a miracle too, full of love and respect. And you are a miracle, Rozia. You survived against all odds. That is something to celebrate. You survived. You beat Hitler. You will carry on. And be happy.*

Friday, December 17, 1948, evening

No one went out today because of the blizzard, which has been raging for two days. We spent the day reading and playing board games. And eating. I was hungry all day, and Eva always seemed to have a plate of something to offer me that I couldn't resist. I ate chopped liver and gefilte fish for lunch, a corned beef and pickle sandwich for a snack, and apples and oranges and nuts in between. And now I'm waiting for dinner!

Oh, the evening edition of yesterday's paper was finally delivered (late, because of the blizzard) and we found out that the young prince has been named Charles, or as they called him, Bonnie Prince Charlie.

Sunday, December 19, 1948

The roads were finally opened today, and I was able to take the bus to the Y. I was still tired and still trying to understand what happened to me after the play, and why. I told Oskar everything. He gave me a big hug and said that I'd been so lucky — to see my family like that. Sometimes he dreams of his family, but it is usually nightmares of their deaths.

And then he said, "And Jewish people do have hope, because we trust in God even though we know that horrible things happen that we don't understand. Don't forget, when we say the prayer for the dead, the prayer is all about life, and we praise and thank God." I know he is right. I know the prayer for the dead by heart.

I suppose I could look at things two ways.

One. I am the unhappiest, unluckiest person in the world because my family was murdered and I was left all alone and I should never be happy, but should spend my life remembering that horror.

Two. The horror will never leave me. But I am the luckiest person in the world because I have a family that loves me, a best friend forever, a boyfriend who is the sweetest boy in the whole world, and a brand new black coat with a white furry collar.

I will choose number two.

Violet Pesheens

These Are My Words

The Residential School Diary
of Violet Pesheens

Flint Lake, Ontario

September 1966 – June 1967

BY RUBY SLIPPERJACK

Violet (nicknamed Pynut) is spending her first winter off the Reserve, enjoying time with her grandma, even if it's just doing chores or going fishing. Life in the village is different from what she's used to. There are challenges, like the scary dog that won't stop charging at her; but surprises too, like making new friends. And Pynut wants to talk with an older girl who is home from Residential School, because Pynut herself will be going there, far from home, in the fall.

Winter with Grandma

Sunday, November 11, 1965

I turned twelve years old today.

Grandma gave me a new diary for my birthday. It has a shiny gold lock on it and tiny little keys!

Oh, here's Grandma coming up the path! The usual packsack is on her back and her long skirt is sticking out beneath the thick coat that she often wears, like all the women here. She has on that blue cotton scarf with big red flowers on it. That's her "going to the store" outfit. She always has her walking stick with her too. Good for beating off dogs.

The first thing I noticed when I moved here is that they dress differently in this village than the Reserve up north where I was living with Mother.

Evening, after supper

Grandma brought home some pork chops as a special treat, so we had a very nice supper. Just now she lit the coal-oil lamp for me at the table. She is reading a book with the other lamp beside her bed. I think she is the only grandparent here who can read and write. She just put the last log into the stove for the night. It is time for bed.

Monday, November 15

The snow was very deep on the path to the school this morning. I got there and found a note on the door — *NO School Today.* I was so happy to see that! I ran all the way home. The big black dog next door came up barking and growling at me again. I do not like that dog, yet I have to walk by him each time I come home. He does not bother me when I am going. It's only when I come back that he charges at me.

I just finished my homework from Friday. It was a good thing that there was no school today.

Tuesday, November 16

Teacher said the oil stove in the school broke yesterday and he had to get it fixed. Too bad it was fixed so quickly. Another day at home would have been nice. At lunchtime, when the black dog came charging at me, he ran into a frozen stump that was buried in the snow. He gave such a loud grunt that I laughed out loud and he came at me again, barking even louder, and he even followed me a ways. I think he didn't like it when I laughed at him. Then I heard Bill yell, "Blackie!" He was kind of late to call his dog!

School was fun today. I like the way the class divided and I love the smell of crayons and Plasticine from the little kids by the window. Since Tall Mike and I are the only ones sitting in the Grade Five row, right next to the blackboard, we have to wipe it and dust off the erasers at the end of each day. Sometimes I wish Tall Mike didn't sit behind me — he never says anything and his knees are always lifting up the top of his desk.

So far, I'm liking my first winter with Grandma. I did not like the Reserve up north where Mother lives. No, that is not true. It's my stepfather I do not like. I love my half-brother and half-sister. Oh! I forgot her birthday was last week — now she's six, just a year younger than him! Anyway, I will have to write to Mother tomorrow. After being here with Grandma every summer, I'm glad I finally talked Mother into letting me stay this winter.

I saw a big beige dog this morning. I had never seen him before. He was sitting on the hill just watching me go by. After school when I came back, he was there again, watching the big black dog charging at me. I just kept walking. Grandma says he probably belongs to the new railway foreman who just moved in to that house on the other side of the hill beside the railway tracks.

Sunday, November 21

I am tired. Grandma and I have been getting our winter wood supply all day. She cut some trees down behind our cabin and then we piled the logs on the toboggan and pulled the load home. After that, we put a log on the sawhorse and then we cut it with a handsaw. It is much easier doing it together, with Grandma at the other end of the saw and us pulling and pushing it back and forth. Then she split the wood with an axe and I brought the split wood inside and piled it in the woodbox behind the door. When the box was full, I piled the rest of the split wood outside, close to the door. The sun was shining and the air was crisp. It was really nice. We laugh a lot when we work together.

Tuesday, November 23

I was coming home after school and Blackie came charging at me as usual, but then the beige dog suddenly came in at full speed and he shoulder-slammed Blackie right off his feet and sent him tumbling over and over. Blackie was yelping and then he scrambled up and ran off around the cabin with his tail between his legs. The beige dog glanced at me, wagged his tail and ran back up the hill. Grandma didn't know what to make of that when I told her.

Blackie did not charge me at lunch or after school! The beige dog still sits on top of the hill watching me go by.

Friday, November 26

After school it was my turn to wipe off the blackboards. Then Tall Mike yelled from the door, "Pynut! Your grandma's waiting for you at the store!"

Grandma was there with two boxes ready to go when I got there. We put them on top of our toboggan and tied them criss-cross to the toboggan so they wouldn't fall off. Then we set off, pulling on the rope, walking side by side. The path is just wide enough for both of us. As we passed by the trapper's cabin at the fork of the path, his brown dog was just bouncing off his chain, straining to attack us. Grandma says I have to always watch to see if the trapper is in the village to get his supplies, and then I must always use the school path. His dog is very dangerous. Then up the hill, sure enough, the beige dog was there again, watching us go by.

Wednesday, December 1

I woke up this morning and I was alone. Then I remembered.

Last night, a man who lives by the lake came up to our cabin and banged on the door. When Grandma lit the lamp and opened the door, he said his wife was having a baby and that it was too soon. The baby was not due to be born until next month.

So Grandma got dressed, blew out the light and went with the man.

I put a log in the fire and made a jam sandwich before I headed off to school.

I came home for lunch and Grandma was *still* not home, so I made another jam sandwich.

When I came in after school, she *was* home and already making supper.

A baby girl was born. Grandma says she has lots of hair.

Friday, December 10

There was a big pile of wood beside our cabin when I got home after school. There must have been about twenty logs! Grandma said it was from the very thankful new father.

The beige dog followed me home at lunchtime. But he did not follow me again after school, just stayed on top of the hill watching me.

Tuesday, December 14

I opened the door to head off to school this morning and there was the beige dog, sitting on the path waiting for me! He walked in front of me until we came to the hill and then he ran off up the hill.

We have been making Christmas decorations at school. There are all kinds of paper snowflakes on the windows, and we made different coloured chain links that we hung along the blackboard. It looks really nice! Teacher tried to make us sing some Christmas songs, but the kids just giggled and laughed at him because he really can't carry a tune! He sounded awful and I tried very hard not to laugh too.

Thursday, December 16

We knew Teacher was up to something this morning. The first thing he did was to put a bucket on the floor at the front corner of the room. Then he was making a grunting sound and creating a scraping noise at the door. He came down the row of seats with a spruce tree, knocking Tall Mike's toque clean off his head as he struggled with the tree to the front of the classroom. He tried to stick the butt end into the bucket, but he kept missing it, and by then the whole class was just roaring with laughter. Finally he got the tree upright and tied it to wires from the blackboard to keep it from falling over. We were all laughing really hard by then!

I saw one at the hospital last year when I had mumps, so I knew that he was making a Christmas tree.

The other kids did not know what he was doing, and they laughed even harder when he poured water into the bucket. Then he pulled out a big box from under his desk. From the box, he started handing out different coloured shiny balls and the kids were shaking them, not knowing what they were, and then *ping, ping, ping* they started breaking in their hands. Teacher had to explain that they were to be hung on the tree branches. That was very funny!!

Friday, December 17

We kept seeing faces at the windows all morning at school. Mothers were looking inside to see the tree that all the kids were talking about! They were making faces, squinting and shading their eyes to see inside. It was really funny when another face popped up at the window! I was laughing so hard, I couldn't write! We were supposed to be writing a big test that I had been studying for, but I couldn't concentrate every time another kid squealed with laughter as another face popped up at the window. Finally Teacher came and collected the papers, saying that we would write the test this afternoon.

Monday, December 20

I had a good mark on the test!

Grandma and I went ice fishing this afternoon. Teacher let us out early because he had to catch the train back to his home somewhere in the south. We headed out along the shoreline, following an old trapper's toboggan trail. But we stopped by a rock cliff along the way.

Grandma cut two holes in the ice with her chisel while I went to the shoreline to cut some spruce boughs to sit on. I also cut two sticks for our fishing poles. Grandma caught one trout and then we went to shore and built a fire. In a short while, lunch was ready and we had nice hot tea with our bologna sandwiches. After that, we packed the lunch box away again and went back to fish some more. I got one big trout and then Grandma caught another one too. Three trout! I had a lot of fun but I was tired coming back.

Wednesday, December 22

The four Residential School kids got off the train this afternoon. Their families were there at the station to meet them. They are home for Christmas. There are three girls and one boy. They are all in their teens and they are dressed differently from us. The girls have long coats that button up at the front and they are wearing skirts, beige stockings and short boots. Those boots are not going to be very good here with the deep snow! The boy wears a short coat and black slacks and his boots are short too.

They came into the store where Grandma and I were. They looked very smart and I got shy when one of the girls came and spoke to me. Her name is

Emma and she is Tall Mike's sister. She said, "Hello, Violet. So, you're living here now." I replied, "Yes, I live with Grandma now."

It was strange to be called Violet, but I guess she doesn't know me well enough to call me Pynut, like everyone else here does.

After the parents picked up some groceries, they all headed for home. Emma's cabin is at the other side of the train tracks. Tall Mike wasn't there to meet her. He probably had to babysit his younger sisters.

Maybe I can go and visit Emma. I want to find out about the Residential School, because if I pass my grades this year, I will be going to it in the fall.

Thursday, December 23

I went to visit Emma this afternoon. Her dad had to buy her a pair of high winter boots and thick pants. There are lots of kids at her house. She is the oldest and then there's Tall Mike and two brothers, Jimmy and Ken. The boys are in Grade Two and Grade Four in our classroom. Then there are the two little girls. They are two and four years old. Emma is fifteen years old and she has been in Residential School for two winters.

Her mother gave us a slice of bannock with butter and jam to go with our tea. She's nice. I see her at the store sometimes.

Tall Mike wasn't there. Emma said that he went

to get firewood with their dad. I could see why Tall Mike never gets his homework done.

I didn't get much chance to ask Emma any questions, so I invited her to come and visit me before she goes back to Residential School.

Saturday, December 25

It is Christmas today. But nobody celebrates Christmas here and no one gives presents. Grandma gave me a bag of Christmas candies for a treat anyway. They were all in colours of red, green and white. There were some that looked like a wavy ribbon. Oh, they were good! I will try to make them last a long time.

Tuesday, December 28

Emma showed up at the door just after supper today. We sat at the table and Grandma served us some cookies with our tea. Grandma asked more questions about Residential School than I did. Emma told us that I was not to dress in new clothes to go there, as they are taken away and burned the minute you arrive. I would be given other clothes that were the same as all the girls in the Residential School. My hair would be cut the same as hers — just below the ears, and she has bangs. They are not allowed to wear pants, only skirts or dresses. There is a bell for everything. When to get up, when to get dressed, when to go downstairs for breakfast, when to get your coats on for school. Then you have to walk to a city school together. The same thing happens when you get back. There is a bell for supper, cleaning up, homework, television and then bedtime.

I don't think I will like the place. Emma will be there though. That is, if they send me to the same place. I could be sent somewhere else too. Everyone knows that some kids have died running away from those schools, trying to get home. So, that was not an option.

January 1, 1966

Grandma warned me last night that there would be gunshots going off at midnight. I wasn't prepared for the noise that woke me up though. Every person who owned a gun — which was pretty much every man in a village of hunters — shot off their gun into the sky! Then today is the "hugs and kisses" day. People go around from cabin to cabin, hugging and kissing everyone. I don't think I want any smooches from old fogies. Grandma and I smiled at each other at breakfast and decided to go ice fishing for the day.

Oh, too late. Here comes Ol' Moses!

Moses just left. He hugged and kissed Grandma and Grandma kissed him back on the cheek. She was making faces at me over his shoulder. I got a hug and kiss too but I did not kiss him back. We are going to hurry and pack our fishing stuff before someone else comes.

Friday, January 7

Grandma came home from the store and she says that the new foreman's family got off the train. She says now she understands why the beige dog took so much interest in me. The girl is about my age, same height, same weight, same long black hair to the waist, and no bangs. Grandma even said she has her hair parted down the middle like mine and braided at the back. The only thing, Grandma says, is that her nose is a little big and she has very black eyebrows, and they do not speak Ojibwe! I hope I see her at school on Monday.

Monday, January 10

Sure enough, the girl and her brother arrived at the school and they were introduced to the class. Her name is Jennie and her younger brother is Jack. She sat down in the desk in front of me. We are in the same grade too! Jack sat in an empty seat behind Jimmy in the Grade Three row. At recess I told her my name was Violet, and we spent the time talking by the doorway. The kids were running around chasing each other to the outhouses and back again. We saw Jimmy throw Jack into a snowbank and keep pushing him down when he tried to get up. Jennie made to go and help, but I held her back because I caught sight of Tall Mike striding up to Jimmy and yanking him off his feet by the back of his jacket collar. Then Jack took off around the corner of the school.

Wednesday, January 12

Yesterday Jennie wanted to know why people call me Pynut instead of Violet. She laughed when I told her that there is no *V* or *L* in the Ojibwe language. I spent a lot of time with Jennie and her beige dog, Chuck. She explained to me that he's a purebred Labrador retriever. I had to ask Grandma how to spell that word, and I had no idea that there were such things as purebred dogs. I felt stupid.

We spend a lot of time playing cards at her place. I can't get over how close her house is to the railway tracks. The kitchen cupboards rattle each time a train goes by. The house is made of boards, like everything that is owned by the railway. I asked Jennie how she can sleep at night when a train goes by. She said she was used to it and sleeps right through. We walk together from school where the path from the hill joins mine down below. At lunch and after school, the dog is always there on the hill, waiting for Jennie, and he comes running down when she gets there and runs home with her beside him. He really loves that girl. He doesn't pay much attention to me now that Jennie is back with him.

Wednesday, January 19

At lunch today, Jennie came running into our cabin crying. Chuck got hit by a train and he is dead! There was no one home when Jennie found the dog.

She was so upset that Grandma had to walk her home when she thought Jennie's mother should be back from the store. Jack was probably helping his mother with the groceries.

I cried too. Chuck was a wonderful dog. He was the only dog that I had ever got to know. I told Teacher what happened to Jennie's dog when I got to the school.

Just got home

I am still shaking. I can hardly hold my pencil. Grandma is not home. I found a note saying she has gone to check her rabbit snares. I will start from the beginning.

I heard the train come in after lunch and I was waiting for a letter from Mother today.

So after school I ran into the store and down the back to the mailroom, and, sure enough, the clerk handed me a letter from Mother. I was so excited that I ran out of the store and down the hill. As I ran by the trapper's shack, his brown dog lunged at me, all teeth, and he landed on my back and knocked me down into the snowbank. I could feel his massive jaws clamping down onto my parka hood! Then suddenly his weight was off me and a dogfight started behind me.

I scrambled up and saw that Blackie was down on the ground, fighting for his life, and I got to my feet and ran to Blackie's cabin screaming for help and by then, I met Bill and he had a piece of wood in his hand. My knees collapsed at his porch step and I turned to see that the trapper was now pulling his dog by his broken chain. I watched Bill pick up his poor dog and he brought him home and set him down in front of me.

Blackie was just trembling from head to foot and his head was drooping down. I put out my hand and stroked his head while Bill checked him over. Finally he said, "No harm done. He has such thick hair that he's probably just bruised."

I told Bill that Blackie saved my life. He just looked at me and said that Blackie is always just all noise and had never been in a fight before in his life.

I was *so* scared!

Friday, January 28

Jennie did not come back to school until a couple days ago. Now she has a new puppy. It is another purebred beige Labrador retriever and her name is Lucy. She is three months old. Her uncle from her hometown had just got the puppy when he heard about Chuck, so he decided to give it to her.

We have a lot of fun with her, and Jennie is still trying to train her.

Grandma doesn't like it when Lucy leaves a puddle on our floor, so I spend a lot of time at Jennie's house. It is really strange that Blackie now greets me with his tail wagging and follows me a little way when I come and go past his cabin. It's like he is escorting me safely through his property.

Saturday, February 5

Grandma and I took the early train to town. They always have rummage sales on Saturdays at the church and Grandma wants some fabric that she can get from full skirts and dresses. When we arrived at the church, we went down a dark set of stairs and there were a lot of women there. I held a paper bag while Grandma shoved whatever she picked into the bag. Then we went to the table by the door where a woman stood. She was very nice and she emptied our bag and counted up the cost and Grandma paid her. We caught the afternoon train back.

Sunday, February 6

When we got home yesterday afternoon, Grandma unravelled some full skirts that had yards of fabric on them, and washed them and the two flannel sheets she had bought. I hung them out on the line for her. This morning, I watched her fold one of the flannel sheets and one of the skirts, which was now just yards of green fabric with little yellow flowers. She said the young mother she'd helped would make something out of that, and the sheet was for the new baby. She put them into a bag and left to deliver her gift.

I am sitting here thinking.

Chuck saved me from Blackie. Then Blackie saved me from the trapper's dog. Now Blackie is my friend.

Jennie told me that her dad had paid a lot of money for Chuck, and I guess her uncle did too for Lucy. I do not understand. Puppies get killed here when no one wants them. Otherwise there would be too many dogs that belong to no one and have no one to feed them.

Then I thought of Grandma sharing the little she could afford from the rummage sale.

Everyone here has no money. They hunt and trap to feed their families. There are the fortunate few men who work on the railway. I wonder just how much Lucy cost.

I am realizing that life is a very complicated thing.

Triffie Winsor

Flame and Ashes
The Great Fire Diary of
Triffie Winsor

St. John's, Newfoundland
June 1892 – September 1892

By Janet McNaughton

Half a year after a huge fire destroyed her father's business premises as well as their house, Triffie and her family are trying to find ways to make their rough lodgings more like home. But it's hard when Christmas is coming and she knows this one will be far different from last year's celebrations. Still, Triffie, her friend May, and even her brother Alfie decide to make Christmas memorable, at least for someone who's less fortunate than they are.

✿

Raffle Mania

Wednesday, November 9th, 1892

Last night, I dreamed of Christmas morning in our lovely new home and of waking to find a Christmas stocking on my silk jacquard counterpane with an orange and ribbon candy and a pair of cashmere gloves inside. The hall carpet felt soft and clean under my feet and I could hear Mama, Papa and Sarah laughing in the dining room below as the smell of toast and ham drifted up from Christmas breakfast. Alfie called, "Merry Christmas, Triffie!" as he rushed to join me.

Then I really did wake to find myself lying beside Sarah, staring at the raw wooden beams of our warehouse home in the early morning dark and feeling as if we'd just lost everything all over again.

Thursday, November 10th, 1892

Alfie's schoolmaster gives him lots of homework every night, so I have time to write in my diary.

Everyone is trying to be cheerful, but I am dreading Christmas. It seems we've barely progressed since the fire last July. The parts of town that were untouched by the fire are filled with heaps of garbage (or worse). At least the City finally cleared the rubble from Water Street, though it took one hundred men with one hundred carts to do it.

But Christmas will come, so I must fix my mind on the good things that have happened since the fire. Unlike many in St. John's, we have a solid roof over our heads (though it belongs to an old warehouse). Papa's shop on the floor below us is thriving, with twenty clerks and shopgirls now at work. Behind them, rows of tailors and dressmakers fill the air with the cheerful clatter of their sewing machines all day long. Best of all, our new candy kitchen will soon open in a storefront on Merrymeeting Road. The demand for candy at Christmas is boundless, of course, and we have orders from shops all over the island.

That should be enough to make anyone happy, but I still feel crooked. Maybe Alfie has finished his homework.

Friday, November 11th, 1892

We often get past Christmas without snow, but last night we had three inches, followed by torrential rain, leaving the streets all mud and puddles. Today a reckless cart flew past May on King's Bridge Road and she was so busy mopping the mud off her coat, we didn't get much chance to talk before class. But as she passed my desk, she gave me a mysterious smile. I could hardly sit still, wondering what put that twinkle in her eye. At recess we bundled into our coats and rushed outside to talk. The children from St. Thomas's school have recess at the same time, but we don't mix. They seem to think the Church of England Girls' School must harbour snobs, though we've been using their abandoned schoolhouse since September.

May and I walked arm and arm along the Mall (where no carts are allowed, thank heaven) and she revealed her mystery the once. "Aunt Maude visited the school in Bannerman Park yesterday," she began. Miss Maude (as always, devoted to good works) was looking for a poor girl who might benefit from a scholarship to our school. I shuddered at the mention of the park, remembering how Papa's shopgirls, Miss Rosy, Liza and Phoebe, lived in a tent there among many hundreds displaced by the fire until we brought them to live with us. Those who still remain live in mean, low sheds that were quickly framed up last summer. Susie Verge's family is among them. "Did she see Susie?" I asked.

"Yes! That's what I want to tell you!"

May said Susie is working at the school in the park, helping the little ones. I was dismayed to learn Susie is working, but May rushed on to say that both of

Susie's parents are now employed at the new Harvey's Bakery and Tobacco Factory in Hoylestown.

I'm afraid that sent me off on a tangent, and I told May of Alfie's fascination with the tobacco factory, an iron building shipped especially from London, England. All October, Alfie begged Sarah and me (or Mr. Morrissey with his cab when the weather was bad) to detour down to Wood's Cove on our way home so he could watch the construction.

May interrupted to bring the conversation back to Susie, and I was ashamed to have prattled on so about the building. Since the fire, I try to think of those who are less fortunate, but May has much more practice, living in a family of clergymen. Since both of Susie's parents now have jobs, May told me, she may be allowed to return to school. Miss Maude will visit the Verge family this weekend to make the case. "Susie is too clever to leave school without finishing her education," she concluded.

And this is true. Most girls in Susie's circumstances are already in domestic service. But Susie deserves more. She's not a friend (Susie has no friends but her books). I've never seen anyone win so many prizes for her work in our class every year. She belongs in our school.

So there's another cheerful thing to add to my list: Susie Verge may come back to school.

Saturday, November 12th, 1892

The marble candy slabs arrived from New York a few weeks ago and the new candy makers are trained, but Papa is worried. Three of our head candy makers left Newfoundland after the fire to work in New Brunswick. Only Miss Serena Angel remains. She never worked until her father, Dr. Angel, died, and she lives in a world of her own. Before the fire, when we passed the candy kitchen in our old premises, I often heard her declaiming poetry. Today Papa told Mama that Miss Angel went into full mourning when Lord Tennyson died last month. She even made herself black aprons.

After the fire, Miss Angel and her mother took many of Papa's candy kitchen helpers into their fine house on Monkstown Road, so we certainly owe her a debt of gratitude, but no one would have chosen Miss Angel to take charge of the entire kitchen.

Monday, November 14th, 1892

The most terrible thing happened! The new Harvey's Bakery and Tobacco Factory burned to the ground last night! Alfie noticed the flames before the alarm was raised, while he was looking at the harbour through his spyglass just before nightfall. At first Papa said someone must be burning garbage, but the fire grew until Alfie could make out the shape of the tobacco factory. No one knows how it started, an article in today's *Telegram* said. As it was Sunday, the flames got a good hold before the watchmen noticed. All hands tried to save the buildings, but it was too late.

More than one hundred and sixty people have lost their jobs, Susie's parents among them. I wish buildings would not go up in flames as often as they do.

Now the money Susie earns by helping at the Bannerman Park school will be needed more than ever, and she will never come back to school. Today May and I made a solemn vow to help the Verge family have some sort of Christmas, in spite of this calamity.

Friday, November 18th, 1892

May and I spent all week thinking of ways to help Susie's family, to no avail. They will receive Christmas charity, of course, but that's hardly enough. May has one dollar for Christmas presents and I have three, but I'm sure Miss Rosy and Phoebe and Liza will have gifts for me, and Mr. Matt always makes me a toy (a gift I never thought to return until now). Then there's Ned.

Since I found him sleeping in his boat under the wharf, he has become one of the family (albeit one who works very hard). This will be his first real Christmas since his parents died when he was ten — six long years with no Christmas. He's helping to clear the bottom floor of the warehouse, which is chilly work, so I've budgeted twenty-five cents to buy him the best wool scarf I can find.

May and I will have nothing left when our presents are bought. We are despondent.

Monday, November 21st, 1892

What a strange and happy Sunday evening we had! Sarah, Alfie, Ned, May and I were left alone while all the grown-ups went to George Street Wesleyan Church to hear Miss Georgina Stirling sing. They call her "the Nightingale of the North."

Nettie left us a cold supper of roast chicken and it felt like a picnic.

Sarah's making presents so, after we ate, she extracted the solemn promise that we would not peek, under *any* circumstance, and disappeared with an oil lamp down to the shop. May and I soon found ourselves telling Ned the sad story of the Verge family (because we seldom talk of anything else now). When we told him we wished we could help Susie's family, he reminded us that a raffle is the best way to make money at Christmastime. May said yes, but we'd need a wheel of fortune (which Christmas raffles generally use). Ned replied that we could just draw tickets with numbers on them. We were all set to make tickets right then. With the girls in our school and the children in St. Thomas's as well, we'd have a ready-made market at recesses.

Then Alfie asked what we would raffle off.

Nothing, of course. All our trinkets disappeared in the fire last July, along with everything else. Our grand plan came crashing down around us.

· Friday, November 25th, 1892

Today the wind twisted the frame of a house under construction and then the chimney on the house next door crashed onto it. Mr. Morrissey showed us the ruin on King's Road near Alfie's school. All the way home, we passed policemen stationed on corners to warn people away from shaky walls. The wind is still blowing a gale. It feels as if it must have a grudge against us. To cheer us up, Papa proposed a family expedition to the new candy kitchen tomorrow, as it is now up and running, and he invited Ned along. So now we have something to look forward to.

Saturday, November 26th, 1892

Miss Angel deserves her name and I forgive her strange ways, because May and I can run our Christmas raffle, thanks to her.

The new candy kitchen is bright and cheerful, with whitewashed walls and marble tables where the boiling sugar syrup is poured inside tin curbs to cool until it can be worked. Everyone was going full steam, though Miss Angel seems to have it all in hand and she took time to show us around. Near the end of our tour, where everything is wrapped for shipping, I noticed a big wooden crate of broken ribbon candy and candy canes. Miss Angel said those pieces are too broken to be sold, and I had an inspiration.

"Could I have them?" I asked.

"Why, Tryphena, that much candy would make any child quite ill." (She always calls me by my proper name.) I told her I planned to use the candy to make things easier for some children in Bannerman Park, and her eyes filled with tears of sympathy. Papa overheard and placed his hand on my shoulder. "Why, Triffie, what a splendid idea."

I'm sure they think I will give the candy to children in Bannerman Park. It might be wicked of me, but I did not correct them. May and I would not be allowed to run a raffle if anyone knew.

Miss Angel offered to let me use her house to bag the candy, as it is so close to Bannerman Park, and Papa said he'd have it carted to her house along with penny-candy bags that we send out to shops. Then Papa said I was not to venture into Bannerman Park alone and told Ned he could accompany me whenever I need him.

I can't wait to tell May!

Monday, November 28th, 1892

May could hardly believe our luck. We went to Miss Angel's house after school today and made up nice generous bags of broken candy at the dining-room table. Old Mrs. Angel is a sweet woman with a vague, misty air about her, much like her daughter. Then Ned arrived to escort us to the park. Of course, we had no intention of going, but there was too much candy for May to carry alone, so we walked her back to St. Thomas's Church beside the school. (May's grandfather was once deacon there and she knew of a cupboard we could use.)

Since we were passing Bannerman Park anyway, Ned said it might be wise to visit so I wouldn't have to lie if anyone asked at supper.

I knew where to find the Verge family because we'd passed their shed the day we came to look for Papa's shopgirls. The park was bleak in summer, but it's even more desolate now. We found Susie outside with a mousy toddler clinging to her skirts, surrounded by boys playing hoist your sails and run. Susie told us her family now lives in two sheds with a doorway cut between, so they have more room, and they got a stove in October, so that would help over winter. She told us she could even bring the little ones to school with her when her mother was working. She said all this in her cheerful, distant way, sounding like a grown-up. I suppose spending her life in the kind of adversity that would utterly break my spirits has made her that way. We left her with six bags of candy, enough for each child in her family. No one mentioned the raffle, of course. If she wondered what we were carrying, she didn't say.

On the long walk home, after we left May, Ned asked question after question about Susie. I've never seen him so curious.

Saturday, December 3rd, 1892

The week flew by and our raffle is a roaring success. We sell three tickets for 5¢. Our girls have generous pocket money and some spend as much as 10¢ on tickets every day! May says they have "raffle mania," since they can only win 5¢ worth of candy.

The children at St. Thomas's school pool their pennies to buy tickets. We quickly realized the injustice in this, so we now run two raffles, one for each school. We draw five winning tickets for each at the end of recess, behind the church porch, away from the teachers in the yard. (It's lucky that Sarah spends recess indoors sewing for the Christmas sale.) At first we picked a child in Infants from each school to draw the tickets, but that didn't work. Seraphina Lemessurier certainly looks angelic with her blond curls, but we caught her peering into the bag to find her friends' names before she drew. (We had not noticed them writing on their tickets.) Now May draws the tickets herself.

We made $2.00 this week! At this rate, we will have a fortune for the Verges by Christmas.

Saturday, December 10th, 1892

Raffle mania continues unabated. This week we made $2.50. Some girls have had to write *I must not eat candy in school* on the blackboard after class, but no one tattled on us, thank heaven. May and I plan to place all the money in an envelope and slip it under the door of the Verges' shed before Christmas. This is a very sensible plan, though it's disappointing to think we will never know what good our money did.

Tuesday, December 13th, 1892

Today Alfie asked if he might run his own raffle at the Church of England College to help the Verge family. It seems Ned has been talking to him non-stop about the Verges since he met Susie in the park. Now I am all nerves. Some of the C of E College boys are so much older than Alfie that they are preparing to go to university. But he would not stop asking about a raffle of his own, and someone was bound to over-hear if I didn't agree. This means I must sneak bags of candy over to Alfie before school each day.

We had a lovely snowfall though, all fluffy for once. It hid all the mess in the streets and St. John's looks ready for Christmas.

Friday, December 16th, 1892

Running over to Alfie's school made me late for class this morning. Miss Simms was not angry, but she said that next time I will have to write lines. Because of the snow, we almost always go in Mr. Morrissey's sleigh now, so Alfie is dropped off first and I can't bring him with me to fetch the candy himself. Money from the raffle was down this week; we only cleared $1.00.

Alfie, however, made a handsome $2.20, as the raffle is still a novelty at his school.

Sunday, December 18th, 1892

Sarah and I were allowed to go Christmas shopping by ourselves this afternoon! I found a ten-cent novel, *Topsy Turvy* by Jules Verne, which will delight Mr. Matt, and a tartan lambswool scarf for Ned. We did feel disloyal, going into shops on Water Street, but they are mostly just sheds. Our solid warehouse felt grand in comparison when we returned. We splurged on armloads of evergreen boughs men were selling on street corners. Now our warehouse smells like a forest. Christmas is only a week away!

Tuesday, December 20th, 1892

Alfie came toward Mr. Morrissey's sleigh this afternoon with his head down, carrying a letter from the headmaster. He sniffled all the way home while Sarah peppered him with questions, but I knew he'd been caught. I'd feared an older boy might steal his money. Instead, a high-minded one turned him in for gambling! No one has ever spoken harshly to Alfie, so I forgive him for tattling under pressure. He told everything. The headmaster wants a meeting tomorrow with Papa and Mama and Alfie and me, but also Miss Cowling and, worst of all, May, with Mrs. Seaward and the Reverend Mr. Seaward. Mama and Papa are too poisoned with me to even show their fury, which is a terrible punishment.

I have disgraced my entire family.

Wednesday, December 21st, 1892

I felt like a prisoner facing the gallows all day. It was a relief when Miss Cowling finally called May and me to her office. As daylight faded we walked in silence to Alfie's very beautiful school, where our parents were waiting with Alfie and his headmaster. The whole story tumbled out and everyone seemed greatly relieved to learn we had not set out to rob our schoolmates for personal gain. Miss Cowling was especially moved by our concern for Susie.

I expected Alfie's headmaster, Mr. William Walker Blackall, to be the fierce kind of Englishman, but he is a mousy fellow with bright, enquiring eyes. He did demand we refund all the money, but he softened when May burst into tears.

When I explained we had no way of knowing how much anyone had spent on tickets, it was agreed that the money should be given to the Verge family after all. As "punishment," Alfie, May and I are to deliver the remaining candy to the school in Bannerman Park. Then Papa said he was prepared to find work for Mr. Verge, on the condition that Susie is allowed to return to the C of E Girls' School after Christmas.

Papa says he hopes I have learned a lesson. I might have, but it will take time to sort out what the lesson might be. Now, at least, I am fully prepared to throw myself into Christmas.

Monday, December 26th, 1892

Christmas went by in a blur. We marched off to church and came back to Nettie's special Christmas breakfast. After we'd all exchanged presents, Mr. Matt suggested we walk all the way out to Fort Amherst at the Narrows, to make room for Christmas supper. Ned said his scarf kept him very warm. By the time supper was over, I could hardly keep my eyes open.

Today, Mrs. and Miss Angel put on a very grand dinner for the candy makers and their families, and invited us all. As Mr. Verge is now a cleaner in the candy kitchen, Susie's family was there. Ned seated himself beside Susie, but then he was too shy to speak, so I told Susie all about him. Gradually, Susie, in her sensible way, got Ned talking. I think they will be good friends.

As we finished eating, a knock came to the door and we heard a boy sing out, "Will ye have the wren?"

Mrs. Angel invited the wren boys in, carrying their branch decorated with ribbons (and no dead bird, I was relieved to see). They arranged themselves and chanted:

The wren, the wren, the king of all birds,
Was caught on St. Stephen's Day in the firs.
Although he is little, his honour is great,
So rise up, kind madame, and give us a treat.
Up with the kettle, and down with the pan;
A penny or twopence, to bury the wren.
Your pocket full of money, and your cellar
full of beer,
I wish you all a merry Christmas, and a happy new year.

Everyone applauded and the wren boys got pennies *and* cake, quite a haul for them. Old Mrs. Angel was delighted. We don't see wren boys every year and, she said, they bring luck. I hope she's right.

NOREEN ROBERTSON

TO STAND ON MY OWN

THE POLIO EPIDEMIC DIARY OF
NOREEN ROBERTSON

SASKATOON, SASKATCHEWAN
JUNE 1937 – NOVEMBER 1937

BY BARBARA HAWORTH-ATTARD

Noreen, along with thousands of others, has suffered the paralysis caused by polio. Even after she makes a partial recovery, she has had to learn to walk again, using crutches. At the same time, Canada, and the Prairies in particular, are still in the grip of the Great Depression, with farmland turning to dust and men riding the rails in hopes of finding work elsewhere. It takes a strong spirit to keep hoping for the best.

Snowflakes for Christmas

Thursday, December 2nd, 1937, evening

I am in bed in my bedroom in the sun porch, except it isn't *my* bedroom anymore, because Jean is sharing it with me. As Mother says, just when you think things are settling down, something else comes along, and the something else this time is Cousin Jean and Aunt Ella and Uncle Tom moving in with us!

I just peeked over the top of my diary at Jean. She is curled up under the covers of her bed staring at the wall — just like she has done all day! James and Edmund and Mother and I helped Aunt Ella unpack, but Jean didn't get up even once from her bed. I told Mother that I thought it very unfair that Jean was the one moving in, yet *we* did all the work. Mother said to just leave Jean alone for now. I still think it is unfair.

Here is how it happened that Jean is sharing *my* bedroom: After church last Sunday, Uncle Tom and Aunt Ella came to visit us. Their faces were very serious. Dad shooed Edmund and me into the sun porch

— *my* bedroom — and told us to stay there, then he shut the door.

I made Edmund lie down with his ear next to the crack at the bottom of the door because I wanted to know what was going on. These stupid braces on my legs keep me from getting up and down easily, so Edmund was my only choice.

A secret: Mother does not allow me or the boys to say the word *stupid*, but as I only say it in my *private* diary, I don't think that counts as a wrongdoing.

I just peeked at Jean again. Isn't she ever going to move? I wonder how long we are going to have to leave her alone. It's very annoying having a silent body in *my* bedroom. Thank goodness we each have our own beds. Most of Aunt Ella and Uncle Tom's belongings got stored in our garage, but Grandpa and Dad set up Jean's bed and dresser.

But back to my story.

What happened is that Uncle Tom lost his job at the bank but was too embarrassed to let anyone know, so for three months he pretended he was still working. He said he didn't want to worry us, as we had enough on our plates with me being sick with polio.

Jean just sat up and yelled at me to stop looking at her. I told her I was not looking at her. I also wanted to say that I didn't think people who are guests in someone else's bedroom should yell at that someone else. But I didn't. She's curled up on her side again now. I just looked.

To continue, Aunt Ella and Uncle Tom couldn't keep up the payments on their house, so they rented it out, and now they needed a place to live. So they moved in with us and now our house is bursting at the seams. Edmund and James share a tiny bedroom, Mother and Dad have their room, and Aunt Ella and Uncle Tom are now in my old bedroom, which was Grandpa's room. Grandpa is sleeping in the dining room, where I am supposed to sleep in the winter. Mother says that if we leave the door between the porch and living room open, some heat should come in here and Jean and I should be warm enough and that it will be only for a little while. Then she put a tower of quilts on each of our beds.

All I can say is that I'm glad it's been a mild winter in Saskatoon so far this year. And that is the story of how stuck-up Jean is now sharing my bedroom.

Saturday, December 4, 1937, afternoon

Grandpa drove Uncle Tom to the train station this morning. Uncle Tom sold his car and Dad's is still up on blocks in the backyard, as we can't afford the gasoline to run it, so we only have Grandpa's car for the entire family! Uncle Tom is taking the train all the way from Saskatoon to Toronto to find a new job. Grandpa says that the Depression hit Saskatchewan the hardest of all the Canadian provinces, and we all know that there isn't any work to be found here.

The rest of the day was gloomy, inside and out. Inside, because Aunt Ella cried all day, and Jean is *still* in bed, and outside, because it is grey and cloudy and raining.

I helped Mother with the dishes — everyone's dishes — after lunch, and while I dried I told her I thought a certain person — Jean — could be helping. Mother said to just give everyone a bit of time and to be extra nice to Jean. I'll try, but it's hard to be nice to someone who isn't particularly nice to you.

Sunday, December 5, 1937, evening

Ann came over to visit me this afternoon. I was so happy to see her, after living with silent Jean for three whole days. The rain stopped briefly and Grandpa said we should all go for a walk to exercise my legs. He even made Jean get up and come with us, as he said it was better than her moping around the house. She obviously didn't think so. She walked almost an entire block in front of us, complaining that we were too slow. Grandpa told her we were *ambling,* a relaxing kind of walk, but really we're slow because of me and my stupid crutches and braces.

Anyway, we got to the end of our block and turned the corner, and at the first house on the street there was a young couple with a baby and two small boys in their front yard. All their belongings were spread over the lawn to sell! A dining table and four wooden chairs, a buffet and a crib and pots and pans. Grandpa told Ann and me to keep walking and catch up to Jean, but I looked back and saw him take some coins out of his pocket and put them in the man's hand.

When Grandpa caught up to us, he said, "I know that young man. I taught him ten years ago and he was a good student — polite and smart. And now he's out of a job and they're selling their belongings to get rent money." All of a sudden Jean started to cry, turned around and ran back toward our house.

"Unsettling times for everyone," Grandpa said.

We turned around and headed home, too. All the way back, Grandpa muttered and mumbled, then finally said that something needed to be done about the failing economy, and done soon, by those "nimrods" in government. "Just when you think things are bad for you, it turns out there is always someone a little worse off," he said.

(I like that word. I'm going to call James a nimrod next time he bothers me.)

We were all sad for a bit, and I asked Grandpa if he thought there would be a letter in the newspaper in the editorial section from An Old Fogey. He smiled and said we would have to check for the next couple of days. He still won't tell us whether or not he is the

Old Fogey who writes letters of opinion to the editor! But I have a hunch it's him.

Here is a secret: Grandpa told me that Jean ran home so suddenly because she was afraid that her family might have to sell all their belongings, too.

Here is another secret: Just before supper I was drawing the curtains across the windows in the sunporch and I saw James outside by the tree in the front yard. He was laughing with Marcy McCleary! I wonder if she is his girlfriend!

Monday, December 6, 1937, afternoon

I am resting and writing in my diary. Mother thinks I should close my eyes to rest, but Grandpa told her that as long as I am quiet, writing in my diary is a rest, too. It's funny, how Grandpa will scold Mother, like she is still a child. Funny to me, I mean, but not to Mother. She also doesn't think it funny that Aunt Ella keeps telling her how to run the house! *Her* house, Mother says.

This morning Jean refused to go to school even though James said he'd walk with her and show her around the high school. She used to go to a private girl's school, but Uncle Tom can't afford it now. She said everyone would laugh at her because they'd know she was poor if she's going to a regular school. When Jean said that, Mother's nose got out of joint a bit because it sounded like James, Edmund and I should be ashamed to be going to a regular school, but Grandpa smoothed things over and said he would give Jean lessons at home, the same as he does with me.

Here's a secret: I'd give anything to go to school and see my friends. I think Jean is being a nimrod.

Evening

I fell asleep before I could write anything more. Grandpa said my body is still recovering from polio and that's why I am so tired all the time. Well, I wish it would hurry up and go away so I can be better. Sometimes my legs ache so bad it makes me cry.

Here is our daily routine now: After breakfast Jean helps Mother and Aunt Ella to tidy the house while Grandpa massages my legs. Then Jean and I go to school at the dining-room table.

After lunch Jean and I have to go for a half-hour walk — just the two of us. Grandpa says it will be good for us to spend some time together. "You're cousins," he said. "Family is important." Jean and I made a face at each other when he said that.

I remember when I used to tell Mother that I wished I had a sister instead of James and Edmund. Mother said to be thankful for my brothers. I think she said that because she and Aunt Ella fought a lot when they were young and they still fight now. Mother says Aunt Ella is bossy.

On our walk today, the tip of my crutch got stuck

in mud and I stumbled. Jean caught me before I fell. I felt I should thank her somehow, so I told her that I saw James with Marcy McCleary. She was very interested and wanted to know if Marcy was a peppy girl. I asked her what a peppy girl is. She said a peppy girl is full of fun and is happy and likes to go out places. She said men don't like quiet girls. She also said that you can take a medicine called Lydia E. Pinkham's Vegetable Compound to make you peppy, though she has never needed to take it herself. She said that perhaps I should take it. I wonder if I should ask Mother to buy me some.

We walked past the young couple's house, the one that had all their furniture outside, but the yard was empty. I just realized that if they had to sell their belongings for rent money, they probably don't have any money for Christmas presents for their children! That is very sad.

Mother just came and said she'd help me have a bath. I didn't want Jean to think I was a baby who couldn't bathe herself, so I told Mother that I thought I could have a bath on my own. She wasn't happy about it, but said I could.

Before bed

I'm back. I nearly fell headfirst into the bathwater, but managed to grab the side of the tub and save myself. I didn't tell Mother that happened. She would never let me bathe alone again in my entire life if she knew. As it was, she stood outside the door the whole time, asking every few minutes if I was all right.

I forgot to say that on our way home from our walk, Jean and I saw James walking with Marcy McCleary! She must be his girlfriend.

Tuesday, December 7, 1937, afternoon rest time

Mother, Aunt Ella, Jean and I went on a shopping trip after lunch, which I was happy about because it is snowing and cold and I didn't really feel like going for a walk. Aunt Ella drove Grandpa's car to the Safeway grocery store. Mother wanted to drive, but Aunt Ella pointed out that she, Aunt Ella, was older and therefore the more experienced driver. That put Mother in a huff. But then Grandpa told Aunt Ella to please bring his car back in one piece. Mother forgot her huff really fast and all the way to the store Mother and Aunt Ella grumbled about how Grandpa doesn't realize they are grown women with families and that they don't need to be told what to do!

We bought raisins and currants for Christmas baking. Jean and I were in an aisle, looking for baking soda, when a woman came up to me and looked at my legs in their braces and said, "Oh you poor dear," and gave me a nickel! I was embarrassed, but Jean pointed out that I was five cents richer.

Evening

I am hopping mad! I came into the bedroom after supper and found Jean reading my diary!!! I yelled at her and told her it was private. I don't know how she found it. It was wrapped in my nightgown and hidden under my blankets! Aunt Ella made Jean apologize to me. And Jean told Mother that I called her a nimrod in my diary. I told Mother it was my PRIVATE diary, but Mother still made ME apologize! So Jean said she was sorry, and I said I was sorry, but after Mother and Aunt Ella left, Jean said she wasn't the least bit sorry and that it was a boring diary, and I am a boring person. I told her I wasn't sorry either and that I wished she had never come to live with us.

I feel sort of mean now for saying that, but Jean said that she couldn't wait to get out of my stupid (*she* said *stupid*) freezing sun porch.

Wednesday, December 8, 1937, morning

I was so mad yesterday that I forgot to say that I had a letter from Thelma. She is still in the polio ward at the hospital in Regina. She thinks she will be transferred to a Home for Orphaned Children after Christmas. She says that Edna says hello. She also said that she visits Eugene every day for me. She enclosed a letter from him to me that she wrote for him, as he can't breathe very well and is still in the iron lung. In his letter Eugene said that he was doing better, but has to stay in hospital for a few more months. He is sad because his mother cannot come and visit him at Christmas, because she doesn't have money for train fare from Saskatoon to Regina, or to pay for a room overnight. I am so sorry that they all have to stay in hospital over Christmas. I think I'll mail my nickel to Eugene.

Evening

I had planned not to speak to Jean even once today, but then Grandpa had to go out for half an hour during our school time, so he gave us yesterday's newspaper and told us to read the headlines and he would question us on them when he got back. But when he left, Jean turned to the column *Personal Problems*, by Mrs. Elizabeth Thompson. Jean started to giggle and I couldn't help asking what was funny. She told me that a young man had written in with the problem that he couldn't get girls to like him. Mrs. Thompson told him that he was obviously colourless and boring and he needed to make himself more exciting to attract girls. I told Jean that maybe *he* should take the peppy medicine. We both thought that was funny and were laughing when Grandpa got back. I am still mad at her, though.

My diary is nearly full. I hinted to Grandpa that I would like a new one for Christmas, but I probably shouldn't have been so selfish, because there isn't any spare money for a diary. I'll write smaller in it so I don't use the pages up as quickly.

Mother and Aunt Ella are in the kitchen, fighting over how many raisins should go into the fruitcake. Dad just said, "Does it really matter?" They both yelled at the same time, "Of course it matters!" And then they were mad at Dad and not each other. Aunt Ella is upset because she has not heard anything from Uncle Tom.

One funny last thing. At supper tonight, I asked James if he had seen Marcy McCleary lately. He turned beet red. Jean snickered. Mother looked at Dad and raised her eyebrows significantly. Usually that means she wants Dad to give one of us a talking to.

And one last, last funny thing. There is a letter in today's newspaper from An Old Fogey. It says, *In response to your headline* Relief Without Work Bad Policy. *Not every man is an idler, as you claim. In fact, most men would gladly work if work was available.*

We are all pretty sure Grandpa is the Old Fogey.

Thursday, December 9, 1937, morning

I had a wonderful idea last night just before I fell asleep. More later. I have to catch Edmund before he goes to school. I need him to tell Ann to come over to our house this afternoon.

Ann came over after school and I told her my wonderful idea! I want to earn some money to buy a train ticket for Eugene's mother to visit him at Christmas. Ann said it was a fabulous idea and she, too, hated to think of little Eugene alone at Christmas, but then we were stumped as to how to make any money.

So while we tatted Christmas ornaments in the living room (the sun porch is too cold to sit in today) we discussed how to make money. We thought maybe a bake sale, except I am not a very good baker and the ingredients are expensive. Jean was in the living room with us, reading and, I thought, ignoring us. But she obviously was listening because she ended up saving the day!

Here is how it happened: We were discussing whether or not we could get jobs as waitresses. Jean snorted at that idea and asked how I would carry food when all I do is stumble about on crutches. I thought that was mean, but before I could yell at her, she got up and came over to see what we were doing. I told her we were tatting, making snowflake ornaments. I've already made two, one for Mother and one for Aunt Ella for Christmas, and I'm almost finished a third one (that I plan to give to Ann, though she doesn't know it yet). Anyway, Jean said that Ann and I should sell our ornaments. Ann and I looked at each other and got very excited, but then we realized that we didn't know where to sell them. That's when Jean said that we needed to go to where people had a little extra money and suggested that we sell them to the parents and teachers at her old private school. But we were not to expect her, Jean, to go with us because it would be too embarrassing for her. So Ann and I told her we were too shy to go alone, and after listening to our pleading that she come, too, Jean said, "What the heck! I'll come with you." (*Heck* is another word Mother does not let me say.)

Ann and I thanked and thanked Jean. We decided to go next Monday, before the girls spend all their Christmas money.

I must stop writing now because I have to start tatting snowflakes. It takes a long time to make even one of them, and I need to make hundreds so I can make lots of money.

Wednesday, December 15, 1937, afternoon

I have been working so hard tatting snowflakes that I haven't had one minute to write in my diary until now. I'm even tatting in my dreams!

I wanted to write this because it's about polio. Jean and I were doing Math problems this morning when Grandpa slammed down the newspaper and made us both jump. He was upset because there was a report that a nasal spray that doctors had hoped would stop polio doesn't work. It was tested in Toronto, where there is a bad outbreak. "They have to try harder," he said.

Saturday, December 18, 1937, evening

I am tatting like mad while we all listen to a Christmas benefit concert on the radio. A young boy is singing and Grandpa says that the boy had polio like me, but that the polio didn't rob the boy of his voice or his determination to continue doing what he loved. I told Grandpa that it was not school time and that I knew he was teaching me a lesson. Grandpa said I was getting too big for my britches. Jean pointed out that I don't wear britches, and we giggled about that for a while. The boy has a wonderful voice and I am glad his polio didn't take away his singing.

Sunday, December 19, 1937, afternoon

Mother says I can't do any tatting this afternoon as I have been really grumpy all day and I'm obviously tired and need a real rest. I am also probably tired because Grandpa, Jean and I have a secret. This past week Grandpa has been taking my braces off for a short time so I can try walking without them on. It has been a bit snowy outside the last two days and is very slippery, but he and Jean each take one of my arms to make sure I don't fall. Not that it matters whether they hold me or not, because I can only take about three steps and my legs start shaking. I told Grandpa that I didn't want to practise walking anymore without my braces. I'll never walk properly again anyway.

And I'm also grumpy because, after all my work, I only have five snowflakes finished, and that includes the ones for Mother, Aunt Ella and Ann. Ann has four snowflakes done, and I've not even had time to thread green and red ribbon through them yet, and we are supposed to sell them tomorrow! No one will want them anyway. It was a dumb idea. I'm a nimrod.

Mother and Aunt Ella are fighting again. They do this a lot lately. Aunt Ella wants to move the china cabinet to the opposite wall in the dining room to make more room for Grandpa's bed and a Christmas tree. Mother says the tree can go in the living room where it goes every year. Aunt Ella says Mother is stubborn. Here is what Mother said back: "Stubborn? You're calling *me* stubborn when *you* waited so long to tell us Tom had lost his job? That is being stubborn and prideful, and you know what they say about pride."

(Jean just came in and plopped onto her bed. She says she is staying out of the line of fire. I told her that was a good idea.)

To continue, Aunt Ella then said that Mother was always jealous of Aunt Ella's social status. Mother blew a fuse and said, "Why would you take Noreen and me to the Bessborough Hotel for tea when you knew you didn't have any money? If that isn't pride, I don't know what is." Then Aunt Ella said, "Because I thought it would make you and Noreen happy. You'd both been through such an awful time with her illness. I just wanted you to be happy."

Jean just looked out the door. She says both Mother and Aunt Ella are crying now.

I feel so bad because my having polio has upset everyone. Now *I'm* crying. I don't want to write in this stupid diary anymore.

Evening

My ornaments are all done! I can't believe it.

What happened is that I fell asleep before I could put my diary away and I think Jean must have read it again, but it doesn't matter if she did, because while I was sleeping, Mother, Aunt Ella and Jean put the ribbons through my snowflake ornaments and finished them! Then Mother starched them. They look beautiful. Aunt Ella says they look as good as any ornament she's ever seen in a store! And then Mother and Aunt Ella said they were happy to know I'd made two ornaments for them, but they would be even happier knowing that if I sold the ornaments, Eugene would have his mother with him on Christmas Day.

I better get to sleep as tomorrow is the big sale day.

Monday, December 20, 1937, evening

I am so excited I can't sleep. We sold all the ornaments! Ann left school early this afternoon, and Grandpa drove her, Jean and me to Jean's private school. We stayed outside by the front door while Grandpa went into the school to see the principal to tell her what we were doing. While we waited, a group of girls came out and were very excited to see Jean. One girl said, "I thought you had moved! Why aren't you at school anymore?"

Jean looked really embarrassed, so I quickly said, "Jean is moving to Toronto after Christmas, but for now she and her mother are staying with us to help me while I get better from my polio. She's my cousin." (I'm pretty proud of myself for thinking of that entire story right on the spot.)

Then Jean told them that Ann and I had made ornaments and were selling them to make money to help a boy who also has polio. The girls really liked the ornaments.

Grandpa came back and said the principal wanted to buy one of our ornaments, and had given permission for us to show them to the teachers and a few of the girls' mothers who were inside. We sold eight of them right on the spot, and James bought the last one to give to Marcy McCleary for Christmas. (Jean and I asked if he had kissed her yet and he said it was none of our beeswax, but he was grinning, so we think he has.)

We sold them for 20¢ each and altogether we made $1.80 and I added in the nickel the lady gave to me and that made it $1.85. Grandpa said it was enough to buy a train ticket for Eugene's mother and he would see about getting one tomorrow morning.

Here is a secret: I don't think it is enough for train fare from Saskatoon to Regina, but Grandpa plans to make up the difference so that Eugene's mother can go.

Eugene is going to be so excited. And Mother is going to wrap up some of the fruitcake she and Aunt Ella made for Eugene's mother to take to Regina for Thelma and Edna.

Grandpa said he was very proud of me and Ann and Jean for working hard and helping someone less fortunate. It's funny how sometimes I think I am the less fortunate one because I had polio and can't walk without braces, but now I think I'm pretty lucky because I have my family and Ann.

Before we went to sleep, I thanked Jean for taking us to her school even though it was embarrassing for her. She thanked me for sticking up for her.

Thursday, December 24, 1937, late at night

It is Christmas Eve!

At six o'clock this morning the doorbell rang, waking us all up. It was Uncle Tom! He had spent nearly three days on the train coming home to Saskatoon.

First Aunt Ella kissed him, and then she scolded him for not calling while he was away. He said it was too expensive to telephone, but the good news is that he found a job. We're all very excited for him, but it is a little bit sad that Aunt Ella, Uncle Tom and Jean will be moving to Toronto in the New Year.

I spent the afternoon rereading my diary about the past year. I remembered how scared I was in the polio ward here in Saskatoon and then in Regina, but I also remembered all the new friends I made since I got sick. My most favourite part of my diary is selling the ornaments.

It is snowing and blowing outside, and I can hardly move beneath all the blankets Mother has put on me to keep me warm. Next week, after Uncle Tom, Aunt Ella and Jean leave, I will be moving into the dining room to sleep for the rest of the winter. I'll miss my sun porch.

Here is a secret: I might miss Jean, too.

Johanna Leary

A Sea of Sorrows

The Typhus Epidemic Diary
of Johanna Leary

Ireland to Canada East
April 1847 – December 1847

By Norah McClintock

*Johanna lost most of her family to typhus on
the coffin ships that brought them to Canada,
then was separated from her brother Michael, who
had left Montreal and gone ahead to look for their uncle.
She is now busy tending house for Uncle Liam and
her brother, and wants to make a proper feast for their
first Christmas in Canada. But with money scarce,
she'll need to hatch a good plan.*

♣

A Proper Christmas Feast

Can I call something a diary when it is only scraps of paper that I have sewn together? I don't know what else to call this little book, but I do know that it feels so good to have a place for my thoughts again.

I found the pages today while Uncle Liam was helping Mr. Schmidt. Uncle Liam immediately took pity on the man. His voyage took much longer than he expected, and then he fell ill. Now winter is almost here, he has no shelter and he is expecting his family to arrive at any time. Michael does all the chores here and then goes to help Uncle Liam at Mr. Schmidt's. Uncle says that out here, neighbours must help neighbours.

After I finished my chores, I decided to tidy the small storeroom that is piled with boxes that I've never seen Uncle Liam open. I opened them — without Uncle Liam's permission, I confess — to see what was inside. I found a small bundle of letters, some papers with writing on them and — glory! — some blank sheets.

I sat with paper spread across my apron and read the letters, even though they were not addressed to me. There were six of them, all from my gran, each one a few years apart, each one expressing how much she missed her dear Liam and would give anything to see him again. Reading Gran's words made me weep for never knowing her and for the pain she expressed at being separated from her eldest son. Da never spoke of her sadness. I suppose it was her secret sorrow.

The other sheets were scrawled in a different hand. These were lists of food — roast stuffed goose, potato oatcakes, kidney soup, mince pies and Christmas cake — with all the ingredients. I was so engrossed in reading that I didn't notice a shadow fall across me. It was Uncle Liam. I jumped up, scattering the papers all over the floor, and apologized for my long nose. Uncle Liam said nothing, but bent to pick up the papers. He handled the letters delicately, as if he were afraid they would turn to dust in his hands. When he came to the other sheets, he ran his eyes over them and smiled. "I wrote this foolishness," he said.

When I asked why he had written lists of meals, he smiled and I knew I was not in trouble. He told me that when he first came to this country, he often thought of his mother's cooking — how juicy her Christmas goose was, how moist her Christmas cake, how flavourful her mince pies. This was all in better days, before Michael and I were born.

"Foolishness," he said again. "I must have been in a remembering mood when I wrote that list." He would have crumpled the papers had I not grabbed them and begged to keep them. He also let me have the blank sheets.

That night I hatched my plan: I would make Gran's traditional Christmas dinner for my small but reunited family here in our new home. I wish Ma and Da and baby Patrick were here to enjoy the dinner with us. Oh how I wish it! But we're what's left of the Learys now — Uncle Liam and Michael and me — and I will do my best to enjoy it for them.

November 3, 1848

I have received a sign that my plan is meant to be. This morning, after Uncle Liam left for Mr. Schmidt's, Mr. Goodhugh from down the road arrived at our door. Mrs. Goodhugh's most recent girl has left to get married. (Not a surprise, since Mrs. Goodhugh is famous for losing girls. Since arriving in the area four years ago, she has made her way through five girls, Uncle Liam says, all hired to cook, clean and watch the children, and all leaving as soon as they could find more agreeable employment.) This time she sent to England for two young girls whom she can train. Until they arrive, she needs someone to help with the housework and the three little ones. Mr. Goodhugh asked if I would be interested. I immediately offered my services three days a week. We struck a bargain as to my wages. Mr. Goodhugh asked me not to discuss the terms with his wife. (Mrs. Goodhugh is also famous for minding her pennies.)

November 4, 1848

Uncle Liam says he doesn't understand why I would accept more work when there is so much to be done at home. I told him I'd do my best to keep up with my chores here, but that the money I earn will help me plan my future. After all, I'll soon be fifteen and I need to think about these things. I set out early in the morning to walk to the Goodhughs. I am excited about my plan.

November 5, 1848

I am bone weary from chasing little Goodhughs all day long. Agnes, the baby, gets into all kinds of mischief the minute I turn my back. The two boys, John and Simon, make sabres and pistols out of whatever they can find, and wage war. I am supposed to watch them *and* help Mrs. Goodhugh with her cleaning and cooking.

November 15, 1848

Mrs. Goodhugh and the children keep me so busy that by the time I stumble home, I have scarcely enough energy to wash up, do a bit of my chores here and fall into my bed. But it is worth it. Uncle Liam is going to be so surprised when Christmas finally arrives. So will Michael.

November 20, 1848

If I don't write what I feel, it will spill out of me as gossip. Ma always said gossip is a habit to be avoided at all costs, as no good ever comes of it, and it reflects badly on the speaker. It is much better to pour my thoughts onto a page that no one else will ever see.

It is about Miss Cantrell, the horrible woman. She puts on airs because her brother is an important person, a retired army surgeon — English, of course — who settled in the area some time ago. She keeps his house for him and is as haughty as any English person I ever met. She tried to make off with my goose and was rude and unpleasant when I told her she could not have it. I am so angry I could spit.

November 21, 1848

I have reread what I wrote yesterday, and I am ashamed of myself. Even though it is true that Miss Cantrell puts on airs, she was no doubt only acting according to her nature. Like many English, she looks down on the Irish and on servants, and to her I am both.

Here is what happened. Miss Cantrell arrived yesterday afternoon to have tea with Mrs. Goodhugh.

Mr. Goodhugh also saw military service and so Miss Cantrell sees Mrs. Goodhugh as worthy of her friendship. Miss Cantrell is tall and stout, with grey hair and a dour expression. She dresses from top to toe in black. The only bright spot on her entire person is a gold ring set with white and red stones — diamonds and rubies. It is beautiful.

The two spoke in the parlour, a new addition to the Goodhugh house. When I came in with the tea tray, Miss Cantrell immediately fell silent.

I did not think of her again until I stepped outside to sweep the veranda. Mrs. Goodhugh is very particular about her veranda. That is when I saw Miss Cantrell with Tom, Mr. Goodhugh's hired boy. Miss Cantrell was pointing to my goose, which Tom then set about catching. When he brought the goose to Miss Cantrell, I ran to see what was happening.

Miss Cantrell had purchased my goose! When I told her it was not for sale, she stared at me as if I had taken leave of my senses and commanded me to get my mistress. I tried to tell her that the goose was mine, promised to me as part of my wages. It is the fattest of all the geese. Thank goodness Mr. Goodhugh came to see what all the commotion was about. If he hadn't, my goose would have been served up at Miss Cantrell's.

November 23, 1848

Mrs. Goodhugh was in a vile mood all day. She and Mr. Goodhugh argued fiercely about the goose. Simon, the younger of the boys, whispered to me that they have been arguing about it for two full days. Mrs. Goodhugh was angry because of the embarrassment I had caused her — and because I had chosen the best goose. It was just my luck, too, that she caught me listening to her argument. She sent me home. I don't know whether she wants me back or not, but no matter what, I intend to have my goose.

November 25, 1848

I was not sure what to do this morning — go to Mrs. Goodhugh's or stay home and attend to my chores here. They have been mounting up, and I sense that Uncle Liam is impatient. He says that many hands make light work, and there are only the three of us to do everything.

In the end, I went to the Goodhughs' and was astonished when Mrs. Goodhugh apologized to me. She did not know about my arrangement with Mr. Goodhugh. She did not snap at me once today. Nor did she scold me when I burnt the little cakes for Mr. Goodhugh's tea.

November 27, 1848

I am run off my feet, but I tell myself that it will be well worth it when the time comes. It is a grand scheme and I am happy to have hatched it.

December 1, 1848

It is December already, and I am in a panic. I have the goose. I am confident that I can manage the potato oatcakes, the stuffing for the goose, the kidney soup and the mince pies. It is the cake that worries me. I have never made a Christmas cake, and what Uncle Liam wrote down is only what he can remember. What if he has forgotten something? I know already that some ingredients — the spices, the lemon and the candied fruit — will be a problem. Uncle Liam does not keep them on hand, nor does Mrs. Goodhugh (I snooped in her kitchen).

Uncle Liam and Mr. Schmidt went to town, and I went with them to ask at the store about the things I need. The spices are very dear, and some are not available at all. The shopkeeper's wife, sensing my disappointment, asked me what I wanted them for. As I was telling her, Miss Cantrell swept into the store. She nodded to the shopkeeper's wife but ignored me, even though her eyes met mine. Perhaps she is still angry about the goose. Or, more likely, she thinks me beneath her. She went directly to collect the post. She swept out again a few minutes later, pausing only to collect a package from the shopkeeper's wife. Her hands were quite full, but she refused to let anyone help her. I confess that I was envious of the envelopes in her hand. I wish there was someone to write to me.

I left the store with only currants and citrons, the citrons from the shopkeeper's wife's own pantry. The spices I need were not to be had. This was my first setback.

As I left, Miss Cantrell's sleigh passed me. She sat beside the driver — a man who works for her brother — her back as stiff as a board and her gaze steadfastly ahead. Only after she passed did I spot a letter lying in the road outside the store. It was addressed to her and it was from England. I called out, but it was too late. I tucked the letter into my pocket.

December 3, 1848

The letter to Miss Cantrell has been burning a hole in my pocket, so I took it to her today, even though I have so much to do for Uncle Liam.

Captain Cantrell has a fine house. It consists of two storeys, has large windows and is painted white with black trim. It is surrounded by fields and orchards. Captain Cantrell raises horses for sale. He is also an avid hunter. I have never met him.

I hesitated when I reached the veranda. Miss Cantrell has been nothing but unpleasant or aloof. Still, I have something of hers and must return it.

Miss Cantrell herself answered the door. She is even taller than I, and stared down her nose at me. She did not say a word, but waited for me to speak. When I produced her letter from my pocket and explained how it had come into my possession, she snatched it from me. Tears appeared in her eyes as she inspected it. Still she said nothing, so I turned to go. To my surprise, she asked me to come inside.

December 6, 1848

This is the first chance I have had to sit down and write. Today I went back to Miss Cantrell's, at her invitation. I can hardly believe it. Here is how it came about.

When I gave her the letter, her hand shook and she seemed eager to open it. But instead she slipped it into a pocket. She thanked me for coming out of my way. When I said that I knew the letter was important, she looked surprised and asked who had told me. No one, I said, but all letters are important, aren't they? She said she supposed that was true.

She led me to her kitchen. It was large and well stocked, with dried herbs hanging over the fireplace, and little boxes, neatly labelled, on a small shelf nearby. When I stepped closer, I saw that she had nutmeg and cinnamon and allspice. I groped in my pocket for Uncle Liam's jottings and compared the ingredients he remembered to what was in the boxes. Miss Cantrell had everything I needed!

When I turned around, Miss Cantrell was staring at me as if I had grown two heads. "Whatever are you doing?" she asked. She was astonished to discover that I can read, and asked to see what was on the papers. Then she wanted an explanation. When I told her, she looked wordlessly at me. The silence was so awkward that I filled it by telling her my plan. I also told her about the goose. She gave me tea with bread and butter and asked me about my cooking skills. I had to admit that I had never made most of the dishes before. As she questioned me, I couldn't help admiring her ring. When I told her so, she did the oddest thing — she slipped her hand under the table.

December 7, 1848

You could knock me down with a goose feather. Miss Cantrell came calling this morning after Uncle Liam left for Mr. Schmidt's. Uncle Liam is worried what will become of the poor man if his shelter is not completed soon.

Astonished as I was to see Miss Cantrell, I did not forget my manners. I invited her in. She immediately began to empty the basket she carried over her arm, explaining that Christmas cake must be made well ahead of time so that its flavour would be perfect come Christmas Day. She listed everything she would need, and the next thing I knew, we were making the cake together. She muttered to herself about some elements of the recipe. It seems that Gran's Christmas cake is not an English Christmas cake. I held my tongue. If Gran had been anything like Grandda, she would sooner have cut off both her hands than make anything English.

December 10, 1848

My cake is made and set aside to age, as Miss Cantrell says, and neither Uncle Liam nor Michael are any the wiser. This morning I am going to see Miss Cantrell again. She insists on teaching me how to prepare stuffed goose with port sauce (she has promised me some of her brother's port) and mince pies. She says I am on my own for the rest of the menu — potato oatcakes and kidney soup — as she has never made them.

December 11, 1848

Miss Cantrell is not Miss Cantrell at all! She was, once upon a time — before tragedy struck. When she was only a year older than I am now, she married a soldier, the youngest son of a well-to-do family. Her ring is a wedding ring! He was killed in battle, leaving her with a daughter. She allowed herself to be persuaded that the baby should be raised by his family, who could offer the child much more than a poor soldier's widow could.

Miss Cantrell saw her daughter only occasionally over the years, and then the poor young woman died in childbirth. The letter I delivered was from Miss Cantrell's granddaughter, Lucy. Miss Cantrell has seen her only once. Now Lucy is getting married, and Miss Cantrell is beside herself, as she has nothing special enough for a wedding present.

She divulged all of this to me quite suddenly after I told her how I had come to this country. Then she pulled herself up straight, got on with her cookery lesson, and didn't mention her granddaughter again. I feel sad for her.

December 15, 1848

We have had only an inch or two of snow until today. But this morning I awoke to a carpet of white outside the door and a sky filled with lacy flakes falling from an ash-grey sky. It snowed all day.

December 16, 1848

It is still snowing. Uncle Liam and Michael went to check on Mr. Schmidt. They came back after dark to report that his small house is cozy enough, but that he is worried about his family. They should have arrived well before now, but he has had no word of them.

December 20, 1848

Captain Cantrell has been called away and Miss Cantrell is alone — even her hired girl has been given time off to visit her family. I know this because she stopped by to visit Mrs. Goodhugh. When I had a moment alone, I invited Miss Cantrell to Christmas dinner at Uncle Liam's. It seems only right, as she has been such a help in my preparations. She declined.

I took my goose home with Tom's help. It is as fat as can be.

December 23, 1848

I had to enlist Michael to make my plan work. It was his job to keep Uncle Liam out in the workshop while I made the mince pies and prepared the stuffing for the goose. It was also his job to wring the goose's neck. Uncle Liam sniffed the air when he came inside, but did not say a word.

December 25, 1848

The jig is up, as I knew it would be sooner or later. I got up extra early to start roasting the goose and to prepare the soup. When Uncle Liam awoke and came to get his breakfast, he saw the goose and sniffed the soup. I have never seen him smile so broadly. Without a word, he kissed me on the top of the head.

Everyone was in good spirits all day, and the house was fragrant with good food — the goose crackling, the soup simmering, the oatcakes baking and the pie and Christmas cake set out. The house was snug, and the snow stopped falling, although it was deep on the ground. Michael kept trying to steal little bits of oatcake and insisted on sampling the kidney soup, which he declared to be the best soup he had ever tasted. We were about to sit down to our feast when someone knocked at the door.

Six snow-covered people, a woman and five children, shivered in the cold air. They were Mr. Schmidt's long-awaited family! None of them spoke English. I thought, ungenerously, that my family dinner would be ruined because Uncle Liam would insist on taking them to Mr. Schmidt. But that is not what happened. Uncle Liam welcomed them as best he could without their language and seemed pleased to see them. Soon I understood why. He had invited Mr. Schmidt to have Christmas with us because he was all alone in this new place. When he arrived, all the Schmidts threw themselves into his arms and there was much merriment and a few tears.

Not five minutes later, we heard bells. A sleigh pulled up and someone got down. It was Miss Cantrell. She seemed embarrassed when she told Uncle Liam she had been invited to dinner. But once inside, she rolled up her sleeves and helped me with the goose. I noticed that her ring was missing. When she saw me looking at her now-naked finger, she smiled and said that, thanks to me, she had decided on the perfect wedding gift for her granddaughter. It would make the journey to England with a trusted friend.

Dinner was a noisy affair. Everyone stuffed themselves. The Schmidts sang Christmas songs in German. Miss Cantrell joined in — seems she knows enough German to make herself understood! I found myself missing Ma and Da and little Patrick and Grandda so much that I thought my heart would burst from all the sadness in it. But Ma always said that we must count our blessings, not our losses. My blessings are this: I have a new family in Uncle Liam and Michael. I have new neighbours in the Schmidts. And the best Christmas surprise of all: I have a new friend in Miss Cantrell.

About the Authors

SUSAN AIHOSHI is a *sansei* or third-generation Japanese Canadian. Her parents and grandparents were part of the forced evacuation of people of Japanese ancestry from B.C.'s west coast during World War II. As a child, she often heard stories of the hardships her family faced in the internment camps.

KARLEEN BRADFORD has written more than twenty books for young people, most of them novels, from historical fiction such as her acclaimed Crusades trilogy, to contemporary and fantasy. She spent many years living in Ottawa, the setting for this story.

SARAH ELLIS, a former children's librarian, has novels, junior novels and picture books to her credit, as well as a list of awards ranging from the Governor General's Award to the Vicky Metcalf Award for Body of Work. She reviews children's books for major journals, and has served as a writer-in-residence at the Osborne Collection of Early Children's Books.

BARBARA HAWORTH-ATTARD is a Governor-General's Award nominee and the author of thirteen novels ranging from contemporary to historical fiction to the supernatural. She also writes short stories for anthologies and magazines. Whenever Barbara's not writing, she will most likely be reading, quilting or tatting snowflakes.

JEAN LITTLE has published novels, picture books and two biographies — more than fifty books — including the bestselling *From Anna* and *Orphan at My Door*. Jean, who is blind, works with a talking computer when she's writing. One of her two stories in this anthology was inspired by the childhood experience of a relative who sailed from Ireland on a coffin ship and arrived in Canada as an orphan.

CAROL MATAS has written contemporary, fantasy and mystery novels, but is best known for her award-winning historical fiction about the Holocaust and the Resistance during World War II. One of Carol's key interests is drama, a motif which often crops up in her writing.

NORAH McCLINTOCK is a prolific writer of award-winning mystery and crime novels, including the Chloe and Levesque, Mike and Riel, and Robyn Hunter series, but she has always had a keen interest in history and genealogy. She has served as an interpreter at Spadina House in Toronto.

JANET McNAUGHTON has lived much of her adult life in St. John's, close to the neighbourhood that burned down in the Great Fire of 1892. She is an avid reader and researcher, and when she's not working on her own novels — many of them award winners such as *To Dance at the Palais Royale* and *Make or Break Spring* — she teaches creative writing in schools in St. John's.

RUBY SLIPPERJACK learned traditional Ojibwe stories and crafts from her family. She attended Shingwauk Residential School in Sault Ste. Marie for a year, and later, high school in Thunder Bay. She has written five novels for middle-grade and teen readers, many based on her own experiences. Ruby is a faculty member in the Department of Indigenous Learning at Lakehead University. Her Dear Canada novel featuring Violet (Pynut) Pesheens will be published in 2016.

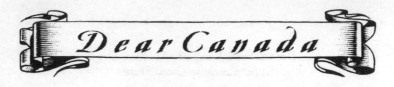

Dear Canada

A Season for Miracles, Twelve Tales of Christmas

That Fatal Night, The Titanic *Diary
of Dorothy Wilton* by Sarah Ellis

*Torn Apart, The Internment Diary
of Mary Kobayashi* by Susan Aihoshi

*To Stand On My Own, The Polio Epidemic Diary
of Noreen Robertson* by Barbara Haworth-Attard

*A Trail of Broken Dreams, The Gold Rush Diary
of Harriet Palmer* by Barbara Haworth-Attard

*Turned Away, The World War II Diary
of Devorah Bernstein* by Carol Matas

*Where the River Takes Me, The Hudson's Bay Company Diary
of Jenna Sinclair* by Julie Lawson

*Whispers of War, The War of 1812 Diary
of Susannah Merritt* by Kit Pearson

*Winter of Peril, The Newfoundland Diary
of Sophie Loveridge* by Jan Andrews

*With Nothing But Our Courage, The Loyalist Diary
of Mary MacDonald* by Karleen Bradford

Go to www.scholastic.ca/dearcanada for information on the
Dear Canada series — see inside the books, read an excerpt
or a review, post a review, and more.